Bird North

Bird North

and other stories

BRETON DUKES

Victoria University Press

TE WHARE WĀNANGA O TE ŪPOKO O TE IKA A MĀUI

VICTORIA
UNIVERSITY OF WELLINGTON

VICTORIA UNIVERSITY PRESS
Victoria University of Wellington
PO Box 600 Wellington
http://www.victoria.ac.nz/vup

National Library of New Zealand Cataloguing-in-Publication Data

Dukes, Breton.
Bird North : and other stories / Breton Dukes.
ISBN 978-0-86473-690-1
I. Title.
NZ823.3—dc 22

Published with the assistance of a grant from

creative
nz
ARTS COUNCIL OF NEW ZEALAND *Toi Aotearoa*

Printed by Printlink, Wellington

To Elizabeth, and to my family

Acknowledgements

This book would not have been possible without the following. Fergus Barrowman and Damien Wilkins. My family, especially Mum and Dad. My friends, notably Kath Dunn and Darryl Short. My 2009 classmates. And – for supporting me with love, rent and critique – Elizabeth.

Contents

Shark's Tooth Rock

Ross wound down the window and looked out to Shark's Tooth rock. Beside him, in the driver's seat, Greg took a pouch of tobacco from his pocket. The only other vehicle in the parking area was a campervan. An Asian couple were in the front pointing at the sea.

'Looks good eh?' said Greg.

'There'll be a current,' said Ross.

'Which one's Shark's Tooth?'

'There,' said Ross.

A long point stuck straight out from the carpark. On the south side of the point the water was sheltered by the steep hills that rose up from the coast road. On the northern side, two hundred metres out and fronted by a long, deep bay, was the triangular rock. A wave crashed over it. If it hadn't been for Greg there was no way Ross would be going out.

'And you're sure there's fish?' said Greg.

'Yeah, but it was a lot calmer last weekend.' Ross wound up the window and went to get out of the car.

'What's the hurry mate?' said Greg. 'Let a man have a smoke. If there were fish last week there'll be fish now.'

Ross took his hand off the door handle and looked at his watch. A seagull dropped out of the grey sky and landed on some rocks.

'I ran one of them over last Christmas.' Greg lit his cigarette with the car's lighter, then pointing it at Ross, sighted down its edge. 'Smacked it with a tent pole and its wing came off.' The orange coil faded. Greg blew smoke into the windscreen.

Ross got out of the car. He'd been back for three weeks. The diving was the only thing keeping him together. At the pub in the weekend he'd seen Greg and told him about the butterfish he'd speared.

'I'll call you,' Greg had said. 'It'll be just like the old days.'

They'd both been pissed. Ross hadn't expected Greg to call.

Greg slammed the door and then slapped his hands on the roof of the car. 'Okie fucking dokie,' he said.

Ross carefully tucked his gloves and booties into the sleeves and legs of his wet-suit.

'You sure you're going to be warm enough? You don't want a hot water bottle?' Greg said.

Greg had the bare minimum: wet suit, fins, mask, and weight-belt. Ross had loaned him some booties and a snorkel.

'It'll be cold,' said Ross.

Greg pulled Ross's dive-knife out of its scabbard. He raised the knife and made the creaking sound from *Psycho*.

'It's for safety,' muttered Ross.

'Yes Sir, Mr Cousteau,' Greg saluted, then picked up the spear and sat on the bonnet of the car.

Ross pulled on his hood and attached the knife to his lower leg. He put his clothes in the car and picked up his fins. The Asian couple were down by the shore. They were taking photos as a ferry passed behind them.

'You know Japanese chicks don't trim their pubes?' said Greg.

'Car keys?' said Ross, holding out his hand.

'When it gets long enough they plait it and tie it with little bows.' Greg lobbed the keys into the air.

Ross caught the keys and put them behind the rear wheel. He stood up. The wind was stronger, and with the tide going out the water by Shark's Tooth was moving like a river.

'We might be safer out here,' Ross said, gesturing at the calm water on the south side of the point. 'I've seen moki.'

Greg was testing the tips of the spear's tines. He shook his head. 'No way mate, and guess who's having first go with the spear?'

The Asian couple stopped their photographing and watched the men make their way over the point. The first man, without a hood and with bare hands, was carrying a spear. His long hair swept around his face. He wore a weight-belt over his shoulder like it held ammunition. The man behind him had a serious look on his face and he didn't react when the taller man pointed at something and laughed. The Asian couple went back to their van. They could follow the men's progress by the birds that flew up from the point.

'Catch you out there,' said Greg, before leaning forward into the water and kicking with his yellow fins.

Ross spat into his mask and worked the saliva around with his finger. Crossing the point, Greg had yahooed about in the rock pools trying to spear small fish. 'You ever had a dose of these?' he'd shouted, holding up a dead crab. Ross sat back in the shallows. There was a gentle swell and he bobbed up and down as he pulled his fins on. It was good to be in the water. At school he and Greg had listened to the same music and played basketball. But that was over four years ago.

Between the end of the point and Shark's Tooth the water was too deep to fish. Without the spear Ross was able to swim it front crawl. The current was not as bad as he'd expected. Maybe the wind had made it look worse. He caught up to Greg, who'd surfaced from a duck dive. 'Save your energy until we get to the rock,' Ross said.

'I just saw a trevally,' said Greg, measuring a length along the body of the spear.

'Trevally?' said Ross. But Greg's head was back in the water.

Ross swam on. The rock appeared. Its face was broad, deep, and bearded with kelp. Fish moved far below like ghost cars on a distant motorway. He duck dived and followed one towards a bus-sized rock formation. He held his nose and blew out. The pressure in his ears eased. Three moki, as plain as commuters, swam by. Ross went around the end of the rock formation. The butterfish was there. It was looking straight at him. Ross made a sound. The butterfish swam off. Ross kicked to the surface. The current had carried him away from the rock and he had to swim hard to get back. Once there he grabbed a piece of kelp and, when a swell came through, dragged himself up the rock. He took off his mask. The wind was cold on his nose and cheeks. He spat and held his hand over his eyes. Greg was swimming towards the rock. He looked awkward in the water, moving sideways as much as forward. Two crying gulls flew towards the coast. Ross sat down and pulled the mask over his face. The last low rays of the sun were shining between gaps in the cloud. A wave broke over the rock. He looked up, and for a moment the world was foam: milk-white and tinged with sunlight.

'This spear of yours needs sharpening,' shouted Greg, treading water and holding up the spear. 'I had a huge fucker on.' He was breathing hard. Ross took the spear and helped him onto the rock.

'How'd you find the current?' said Ross.

'What current?' said Greg, taking off his mask and blowing his nose. His fingers were red and cold looking.

More gulls were flying towards land. On the coast road some of the cars had turned their lights on. Ross slid into the water with the spear. He had to kick to stay in the same place. He looked up at Greg.

'I need to fix something on my flipper,' said Greg. 'You go. I'll follow you.'

Ross let the current take him around the side of the rock. Deep beneath him a large fish swam over a strip of sand. He took a long breath, pulled hard with his free hand and, leading with the spear, went straight down. Small fish scattered like there'd been a bomb blast, and he blew the pressure out of his nose and kicked on. At a certain depth the buoyancy of your wetsuit and the air in your lungs are overwhelmed by the weight of the ocean, and you start to sink. In this way, gliding in with the current, just a car length behind, Ross drew level with the fish.

It stopped and turned. In profile its dorsal fin was a black breaking wave. It came towards him, curious and heavy. He reached out with the spear and let the sling go. There was penetration, and the fish tried to shake the tines from its face. Holding the spear like a hayfork and kicking hard, Ross forced the creature against the rock. The tines went deeper and there was a flush of blood. The fish continued to shudder but with less purpose. Ross needed air. He held the fish and the spear and went for the surface. Long, strong kicks: a trail of blood and bubbles. Dark lightened. The pressure released. He smiled around the snorkel's bit, went through the surface, and took a breath.

'Faarrrkkk!'

He held the fish out of the water. It was a green-flecked black and as wide as a tyre's tread. He retrieved his knife then gripped the fish through its gills and, with the tines still embedded, screwed the blade through the roof of its head. Its eyes pressed, its mouth opened, and then it went still. He freed the fish from the spear and it drooped in his hands. Already the green sheen of its underbelly had faded. He dropped it into the catch-bag he wore like an apron around his waist. A gull called and then another. Further out, attached above the deck of a ferry, two lifeboats were bright and orange.

The current had taken him some distance, and it was a slow swim back to the rock. Greg looked up when Ross called out, but didn't smile or say anything. He had his hands close to his mouth like he was eating a pie. 'Might have that big buttie you saw,' said Ross, grabbing hold of a strand of kelp.

Greg just nodded.

'How you feeling?' said Ross.

'Fucking brilliant,' said Greg, staring at the sea. It was a dark blue spaced with white-capped waves, and he looked at it like it was some awful thing coming through his bedroom window.

'Is that flipper all right?' said Ross.

'Yeah,' said Greg, and then less forcefully, 'I've just finished fixing it.'

'We'll swim straight across,' said Ross. 'Once we get behind the point the current won't be too bad.'

'How's the current?' Greg said.

Ross shrugged. 'If you start getting tired drop your weight-belt.'

'Why would I get tired? Why don't you drop your weight-belt?'

Ross didn't say anything. The fish bumped around his knees.

'Fucking diving,' said Greg. He went into the water holding his head back like a five-year-old. He put his snorkel in, looked down, and then lifted his head up. 'This snorkel's leaking.'

'Come on,' said Ross. 'Let's get going.'

Greg flailed his arms and legs. Ross hadn't realised he was such a bad swimmer. After a few minutes Greg swung around and spat out his snorkel. 'Fuck's sake,' he said. 'Are we getting anywhere!'

'We're going good,' said Ross. He aimed the spear at the place where they'd got into the water. 'Aim there, and you have to go hard or we'll end up . . .' Ross pointed over his shoulder and out to sea. A wave smacked into Greg who coughed and took a breath.

Greg started swimming. Though he had his snorkel in he was rotating his head with each stroke. It was no good. They were going out to sea. I could leave him, thought Ross. I could swim ashore and get help.

Greg stopped swimming. Again he looked around at where they'd come from and where they were going. His long hair made cold black curtains around his cheeks and chin. Behind his mask his eyes were wide. He reached two hands down to his waist and disappeared. Ross watched him under water. Greg shimmied like he was getting out of a tight skirt, and then his weight-belt went free. He bobbed up, spat out his snorkel, and gasped. His lips were blue. On the shore the lights of the cars made long lines around the coast. Ross kicked his long fins. He could see the back of the rock now. The tendrils of kelp were like hair in the ocean and the shore, the hills, and the mountains were curved and still like a dead body in a dark room.

'Ross!'

15

Ross turned around. A court width separated them. The sea was a treadmill. Greg had his arms up. His shout was as feeble and distant as that of a child trapped in a roll of carpet. Ross dropped the spear, unbuckled his weight-belt, and swiftly swam the space between them.

If I leave him, thought Ross, he will die.

The Asian woman was in the back of the campervan eating cheese. The man had finished his meal and was standing out in the wind working his arms back and forward. 'Their car is still here,' he said.

The woman appeared in the van's door. 'What did you say?' she said.

The man pointed to the car. The woman got out and looked.

'Maybe they were swimming to an island,' she said.

The man made a doubtful sound.

'Who would we call?' said the woman. 'The fire brigade?'

Both men were on their backs. Greg was lying between Ross's legs. The fish was squashed between them. With his hand under Greg's chin, Ross had tried to get them back to the coast. He had kicked hard in one direction and then the other. He had shouted at Greg, 'Kick, fucking kick.' But it was no good. The current had them. 'I can't get us back,' Ross said. 'We're better to stay close and save our energy.'

There was no moon and no stars. On the fuselage of an incoming plane a red light blinked red and then green.

Ross could feel Greg's jaw chattering.

When they were still at school Ross used to pick Greg up before basketball practice. Greg would come down the steep steps from his house and stand at the driver's window tapping the glass with a key or a coin. 'You're too careful,' he'd say. 'You drive like you're already dead.'

It had happened like that today. Ross had been so surprised that he'd shifted straight across. A belt loop on his trousers had snared on the end of the handbrake and he'd had to wriggle to get free. Greg had been hooting when he got into the car. 'Good one Ross, real good.'

The current was weaker now, and the sea was less choppy. Ross had lost feeling in his fingers and feet. 'C'mon,' he said to himself. 'Concentrate.'

He still had Greg under the chin. Greg's jaw had stopped chattering. 'I feel warm now,' Greg said.

Ross could see a finger of dark land and a lone light. He unclipped his catch-bag. It hung just below the surface, and before he started his long swim he used two hands to hold it under until it had disappeared.

Bird North

Sheryl followed a grey-haired man off the plane.

The hostess smiled and said, 'Enjoy your day.'

Sheryl nodded and then tipped her head to get the hair off her face. Going up the tunnel she swapped her handbag from one shoulder to the other. Three men in overalls were waiting at the end of the air-bridge. The grey-haired man stopped in front of them and dropped a newspaper into a blue recycling bin. Sheryl went around him and off the air-bridge. There were life sized cut-outs of two muddy rugby players. One player was showing a credit card to the other player as if sending him to the sin bin. The passage opened onto a broader concourse. She passed a man pushing another man in a wheelchair. She'd phoned Marcus at the restaurant the afternoon before.

'Who?' the voice said.

'He does the dishes,' said Sheryl.

The person went away and there was a sound as if the phone were swinging against a wall. There was laughter and then footsteps. They'd arranged to meet at the baggage claim. It was the only place he knew for sure.

Sheryl walked on, watching her shoes and the carpet's

turquoise squares. A man with tinted glasses and a wand stood at attention behind a metal detector.

'We can have coffee,' Marcus had said, in a strangely cheery voice.

There were more people and then a wide window with views over the runway and bay. A lime green plane descended in front of a hill. Sheryl checked the boarding pass in her bag and then, nowhere near the baggage claim, there he was. He had his hands in his pockets and was looking up at an arrivals and departures screen. There were tracks of woolly hair on the back of his neck and the label of his T-shirt stuck out. She touched his elbow and said his name.

He was smiling as he turned around. She shrugged and started crying.

'Sis,' he said, putting his arms around her. She felt his face in her neck. 'Look at you,' he murmured.

They pulled apart. 'I'm only here for forty minutes,' she said, and looked down. The carpet had become a straw colour.

'That's ages,' he said, 'a lifetime for your average white butterfly.' He put his arm around her. 'Been a long time,' he said, as they started walking. The passageway rose and there were more windows, a long coffee bar, and five laughing pilots on stools. The music was like spoons on a roof. A barista with an Afro was shooting steam through milk.

'Somewhere quieter?' she said, and then, 'How did you get here?'

'Bus,' he said, bending to pick up a used napkin. 'A purple one.' He dropped the napkin into a bin and then walked her beyond the pilots and to a window where a child had two hands on the glass. A plane took off and the child slapped the window like there was something out there to startle.

Marcus looked at the child and made his mouth and eyes surprised.

'I'm a machine-gun,' said the child.

They kept walking. Marcus traced the bridge of his nose with his thumb and forefinger.

'You still doing that?' she said, laughing.

'?'

She mimicked him, making her hand go faster and faster like she was trying to start a fire.

'An oldie but a goodie,' he said.

They went past an outdoor clothing store and into the main concourse.

'Over there?' Marcus pointed at a counter. There were panini and pastries behind glass. 'Or . . .' he opened his arms and tilted back as if holding the world. 'Look at this. You could eat at a different place every day of the week.'

She went behind him and sat down. 'Mum wanted me to ask you home for Christmas.'

There were crumbs on the table. He sat down and started rounding them up.

'*I* wanted to ask you too.'

He started transferring the crumbs to his hand.

'We could have Christmas in Te Anau, then go to Queenstown or Alex? Ian's there now. He called the other day wanting your address — he's getting married. Can you believe that?'

Old people were sitting at the next table. There were teapots and cups with saucers. 'This is nice,' said one of the men.

'You reckon there's a duckpond?' said Marcus, holding up the crumbs.

She took a breath and sighed. 'What sort of coffee?' she said.

'A short black.' He closed his hand into a fist, brought his other hand underneath, and made a swinging motion and a popping sound as if a golf ball had been struck. 'I'll tell you a story when you come back.'

A small man whose forehead caught the bright lights served her.

'Now we know where Tom Thumb works,' said Marcus when she sat down.

'What about Dunedin? Mum and I could meet you there. I'd get the motel.' She sipped from her cup. There was a red loop where her mouth had been.

In his big hand the cup looked ridiculous. He noticed her watching and, with his little finger off to the side, took a dainty sip. The skin on his hands was dry and sore looking.

She leaned forward and put her cup down. 'What is it Marcus? Something Mum did?'

'Look,' he said.

Two toddlers were pulling plastic luggage on leashes. The word *Luggagio* was embossed in yellow on the side.

'Crazy,' she said, sitting back. 'This whole thing is absolutely crazy.'

He lifted her coffee cup and took the napkin. He made it into a tight ball and, looking at her in a sideways way and, holding the sleeve of his T-shirt up, he rolled the napkin down his hand, forearm, and elbow so it disappeared into his armpit.

She laughed and put her hand under her nose. There were tears in her eyes again.

'Eh?' he said. 'Who says I haven't still got it?'

Two security men in powder blue trousers walked past.

She looked at her watch. 'I'd better go.'

They hugged near the back of the queue to the metal detector. 'Will you think about it?' she said, backing away.

He made a grand wave as if she were already at the rear window of a rapidly departing train.

21

★

Marcus watched out the window as they drove around the south shore of Lake Te Anau. Bird was driving and telling the story behind his nickname.

'There were three of us in the chopper. I was in back with the rifle, while Bill Nevis spotted and helped truss the carcass. Shanksy would get me in as close as he could and I'd shoot them right out the door.'

Marcus shifted in the seat. 'Is Ian coming next weekend?'

Bird finished drinking from a plastic bottle and lodged it back between his legs. 'This one time the bloody rifle jammed. Now we're talking a hundred and fifty dollars worth of animal. So what does a man do next?'

Marcus shrugged, tracing his thumb and forefinger up the bridge of his nose.

'I got John to bring me right in over her, and then . . . ' Bird jumped his hand off the steering wheel and onto the handbrake between them. 'Right onto its back. Broke one of its forelegs and got . . .' He raised the leg of his running shorts. On his inside thigh there was a cheerio-red raised scar. 'Antler took a wee nick. Missed all the good bits though.'

Marcus felt the hard tip of Bird's little finger press against his thigh. 'I've been Bird ever since.'

'Dad wants me home by three o'clock,' said Marcus. 'To do the lawns.'

'5.6k to Brod Bay then 8.2 up to Luxmore Hut. They still teach maths at school or is it all that sex education these days?' Bird put the car through a tight bend. Marcus held the door handle, pulling himself into the window. The road dropped down and then straight up. 'Watch your guts,' said Bird.

On a grassy slope beside the lake there was a tent and a bike against a rubbish bin. A man was squatting in front of the tent brushing his teeth. 'I'll let Bill know when we get back,' said Bird. 'No. Camping. By. The. Lake.'

The road led them away from the lake. A cow was on the wrong side of a fence. A smear of black fur broke the centre line where a possum had been crossing.

'I've known Bill most of my life,' said Bird after a while. They rounded a corner and Bird leaned across. Marcus felt Bird's ear brush his shoulder. 'Bill Nevis,' whispered Bird, 'our local . . . pig.' He puckered his lips and blew out the last word as if making a kiss.

Ian had said that Bird knew his stuff, that he'd been a national champion. It'll be hardcore, he'd said. It had sounded good to Marcus. But now bloody Ian had piked out and he was stuck with this old guy who wouldn't shut up.

'You got a nickname?' said Bird.

'Not really,' said Marcus.

'Hands, that's what they should call you. Look at those mitts.' Bird held up his left hand as if he were a traffic cop.

Marcus made a small laugh and looked out the window. When he looked back he said, '27.6km return.'

Bird didn't say anything. The breath through his nose was firm. His hand was still there. Reluctantly, Marcus reached over.

'There you go,' smiled Bird, 'you've got bigger hands than me.'

Ahead, on the side of the road, there was an AA sign: Kepler Track.

'In the glove compartment,' said Bird, raising the indicator.

Marcus opened the compartment. There were papers, a manual, a torch, and a jar of Vaseline.

'That's the one,' said Bird, when Marcus traced his fingers over the blue label. He picked up the little container. The white lid had snared a greasy pubic hair. He dropped the container back in the glove box and wiped his fingers on his T-shirt.

'What?' said Bird, 'you never heard of runner's dick?'

They turned onto a gravel road. In the wing-mirror Marcus could see a haze of dust and farther back, in a paddock, an abandoned tractor.

'Looks like it's just you and me,' said Bird, as they pulled into the empty parking area. Bird spun the wheel hard and jerked up the handbrake. The car swung to a stop, causing a sheep to spring back and dash over a hill. It was good to be out of the car. There was a low fence marking the edge of the carpark. Marcus went to it and started stretching. When he turned around Bird was coming towards him, putting what looked like a sock into a small pack. 'Which one's yours?' said Bird, gesturing across the lake.

Marcus looked for a moment and then pointed. 'The lime-green roof.'

The houses were huddled down by the lake-front as if they'd been raked there.

'How does a man come to be living in a house with a lime-green bloody roof?'

Marcus shrugged.

'The only lime-green roof in Te Anau. Has to be a woman's doing.'

'Ian said you won the national champs,' said Marcus.

'Vaseline,' said Bird, holding out his hand.

Marcus had left it in the car. He shrugged again.

'There something wrong with your neck?' said Bird, bouncing his shoulders up to his ears.

'It's in the car,' said Marcus, thinking of the pubic hair and feeling more comfortable out in the open.

Bird went still. This time he held out his hand palm up. Marcus didn't move. It didn't feel right, but he didn't know what to do. He went back to the car.

'It's probably the only lime-green roof between here and Auckland city,' said Bird, scooping out a wad of the jelly. Marcus looked away and started stretching. He was aware of Bird's arm moving in a milking motion. 'Sure you don't want some?' said Bird. Marcus shook his head. 'Right then,' said Bird, zipping the Vaseline into his bag, 'who's setting the pace?'

Marcus was nearly at the bottom of the mountain. He was knackered. A sharp pain had started behind his knee and the ends and tops of his toes felt smashed and blistered. He'd led out hoping that a fast pace would shut Bird up. But Bird – though he wasn't much to look at with his belly and short arms – had stuck with him easily, keeping up the chatter all the way to Brod Bay. There the talk had stopped and at a small bridge, without a word, Bird had gone ahead. And he'd kept going ahead. When Marcus broke the bush line he'd seen Bird high up the mountain, gliding through the tussock and getting farther ahead the higher he climbed. Ian said Bird was a hard bastard and that he knew his stuff, and yeah, maybe he could run, but the only thing Marcus had learned was how to follow someone up and then down a mountain. Then there were all the questions and that thing with the Vaseline. He was going to kill Ian.

He recognised a forked tree from the start of the climb. Then the turned-over wooden pest trap with its wire door and piece of carrot. There was a tight bend, the bridge, and then, thank god, the long decline back to the Brod Bay shelter and the lake shore. He saw movement in the shelter, and then a person came down the front steps: white T-shirt, purple polyprops. At the Luxmore Hut – there'd been cloud covering the mountain's peak and two girls with red and white flags on their packs sharing a cigarette on the deck – Bird had told Marcus that he'd see him back at the car.

'If you thought I was fast coming up . . .' But there he was, standing in front of the shelter. A drink bottle in one hand and something white in the other. Marcus waved, but Bird didn't react. Probably can't see me, thought Marcus. The stupid old bastard.

'Look who decided to join us,' said Bird, when Marcus got to the shelter.

'I thought we were meeting at the car,' said Marcus, between breaths. The light was dim and the air cool. It was good to have stopped. He put his hands behind his head.

'I'm going to show you Marble Hole.'

'I better get home,' said Marcus. 'For the lawns.'

'It's five minutes around the lake,' said Bird. 'C'mon.' He started walking and then stopped and turned. 'Did you want a ride? Or were you going to run home from the carpark?'

The township and the farmland around the township and the high grey sky were all reflected in the lake. Bird threw a stone and then gave one to Marcus. 'Cheer up boy,' Bird said. 'You did okay.'

Marcus threw the stone. It went well beyond where Bird's had landed.

'What is it they say these days?' said Bird, starting around the lake, 'promise? You've got promise.'

Marcus was slow over the rocks. His toes hurt and his legs were tired. He wanted to go home.

Ahead, a fallen tree made a bridge between the lake and the bush. Beyond that the shore disappeared into the bank and the branches of the beech trees dropped their leaves on the lake's surface. The white sock was tucked into the waistband of Bird's shorts. Gross, thought Marcus, he must use it for sweat.

A helicopter was landing on the other side of the lake. Bird climbed onto the log. 'That's what I'd be doing if I was your age,' he said, pointing to the helicopter. Then on all

26

fours, and still talking, he crawled under a low branch and back into the bush. 'It's a man's job that is.' He stood and went a few more metres into the bush and then stopped. 'Marble Hole,' he said.

It was an effort for Marcus to get over the log and then onto his hands and knees. There was the last of the lake stones, a layer of leaves and rotten branches, and then a carpet of moss. It was soft under his hands and if Bird hadn't been there he might have lain down and looked into the trees.

'What did I tell you,' said Bird, gesturing with a flick of his head.

Marcus stood and went around a stump, past Bird, and to the edge. It wasn't so much a hole as a crater. The floor and sides of it were lined with more moss. It was perfectly round and the right size for a merry-go-round. 'It's like a skateboard bowl,' said Marcus, looking back at Bird, 'or a bunker.'

Bird had his hand behind his back as if there were an itch. A fantail was making an announcement. 'What caused it?' asked Marcus, watching the bird go off the branch, up, down, and over the crater.

Bird didn't answer. Marcus felt the moss shift and turned around. Bird was right there. The sock was a mitten over his hand and wrist. The blade of a knife stood through the sock's toe.

'It would be a lot better if I didn't have to use this,' said Bird.

Marcus put his hands up. 'Eh?' he said.

'Turn around,' said Bird.

Marcus didn't move. He tried to smile.

Bird made his eyes wide, and then raised his knife hand as if he had an axe.

Marcus turned. He felt Bird's hand on his back and then he was falling. The crater's moss was wet and even denser.

Marcus started to get up, but the knife pressed into the hard area behind his ear.

'Stay on your knees, but turn around,' said Bird.

As he turned the knife point tracked under his ear and around his neck. He saw Bird's old shoes with their duct tape and different coloured laces, and when he looked up there was the knife and Bird's penis. It was pointing straight ahead, and as Bird wriggled his shorts below his knees it swayed side to side.

'Eh?' said Marcus again.

Bird cleared his throat. 'Most of the Vaseline would have rubbed off,' he said. He spat and then moved forward.

Marcus closed his mouth. It went into his top lip and then greasily up beside his nose. There was a strong smell.

'Ooops,' said Bird.

The blade of the knife was flat on his cheek bone. It shifted so the sharp edge rested under the curve of his eyeball. 'It wouldn't take much out here,' said Bird.

Marcus opened his mouth. He felt Bird's hand on his forehead.

'Easy there,' said Bird. 'Bring your lips back.'

★

From her position on the lime-green roof Sheryl could see all the way to the end of the street. There was an old red car coming. She crossed her fingers. On the phone Marcus had said he was thinking of buying a car and getting the ferry after his shift, though he'd said something similar the Christmas before.

'It's a hell of a long drive,' she'd said.

'Piece of cake,' he'd said.

It was a beautiful Christmas Day. The sky's only clouds were thin and high and tailing away above the peak of

Mount Luxmore. Sheryl was sitting on the ridge of the roof with her elbows on her knees. It was hot and every now and then a drop of sweat dripped from the end of her nose and onto the corrugated iron. She wasn't getting off until he arrived.

The red car stopped five houses up. A woman got out and went to the back of the car. She brought out a box and two shiny balloons attached by long ribbon floated into the air. The woman was smiling as she closed the door. She turned and crossed the street. The balloons were long antennae over her head.

Sheryl's mum was inside. They'd eaten breakfast and then walked to the lake. There were new yellow kayaks and jetskis and children with boogie boards and another child screaming on the shore because a man couldn't get a kite to fly. Sheryl and her mum had an argument about Marcus buying a car.

'He better get something road-worthy.'

'He's a dishwasher.'

'What if something happens on the way down?'

'Jesus Christ, Mum!'

They'd walked home slowly after that, one after the other like mountaineers gapped by a length of rope.

When Sheryl got back to the house her mum had opened two bottles of beer and they sat with the ranchslider open so they would hear his car. The kids next door were chanting and her mum got up and went onto the deck. 'Lucky beggars,' she said. 'They've got a new trampoline.'

Sheryl took her beer to the sink and looked over the driveway. She stood there for a long time. When she turned around her mum was asleep in a chair. She went out to the end of the drive and looked up the road, but she couldn't see enough. That was when she'd put the ladder against the house and climbed onto the roof.

An old man was driving down the footpath on a mobility scooter. As he got closer Sheryl could see there was mistletoe attached to the scooter's front basket and that the man was wearing a fake beard and that he was in fact not old at all. He disappeared behind the neighbours' hedge and then there he was, going past the end of their driveway, steering with one hand and holding a bottle of rum in the other. He went behind the house and she turned and waited for him to reappear. There was the electric whirr of that scooter, the far away buzzing of a jetski on the lake, the children on the trampoline counting in Maori and then all of a sudden what sounded like a helicopter. There was nothing in the air over the lake. The sound was coming from behind her. She turned around. A brown van – there was a giant plastic foot on its roof – was coming down the road.

A block from the house the van's rotoring engine died. With its beaten panels and its foot as a sail it resembled a strange marine craft coasting in to stop and block and be moored at the end of the drive. A man got out. It was Marcus. He smiled at the house and then walked around the van, running his hand down its flank as if re-assuring a horse. Sheryl stayed where she was. She wanted him to catch her up there. The van's rear doors opened and then closed and then Marcus was carrying a suitcase down the driveway. Sheryl stood up but he didn't see her. He was grinning at the garden and at whatever was on the deck and probably waiting for the windows to fill with whoever was inside. Just as he disappeared from view Sheryl said his name. She heard his feet stop, the sound of the suitcase settling on the drive, and then standing tall and making giant clown steps he re-appeared. He looked up at her and grinned. She started to cry. He pointed to the van. 'She ran out of petrol.'

There were sounds from in the house and then footsteps on the deck. Sheryl heard their mum say his name and then their mum was on the drive and Sheryl carefully crossed the roof and got onto the top rung of the ladder and with each step down she said, 'Wait for me. Wait for me.'

After dinner Sheryl and Marcus climbed back onto the roof. There were pine needles sitting like pick-up sticks across the ridges and grooves of the iron and Marcus crept over the roof collecting them.

'Careful,' said Sheryl. 'We can't have you breaking your neck.'

They sat side by side. A large white boat was docking at the wharf out in front of the township.

'They do tours on Christmas Day?' said Marcus.

'The glow-worms don't know about Christmas,' said Sheryl, and then, 'You could get a guiding job in the caves.'

'This roof,' said Marcus, kicking his heel down the iron. 'Do you remember?'

'Wouldn't it be better than washing dishes?'

'I said yellow and you said green. You called a family meeting.'

'I'm serious,' said Sheryl.

'It was the only meeting we had,' said Marcus. He'd bunched the needles, tying one around the others, and now he held them out to her like they were a bouquet.

They were about to get off the roof when they heard and then saw the plane. It was flying fast over the lake. It had a huge nose and many windows. It went up on its side, turned away from the lake, and roared over the house. There was the white underbelly and the black outlines of the various flaps.

'What should we do?' shouted Sheryl. She stood up as the plane banked again and made another sharp turn over the township.

'The pilot must have dropped something,' said Marcus.

Sheryl crouched, looked at her brother, and then sat down again.

Across the road the woman with the balloons came out holding up a bottle of bubbly wine. 'Santa's going home first-class,' she shouted.

The plane made several more loops: going across the lake towards the mountains, then rounding the edge of the lake, before following the road from the start of the track back into town.

The man on the mobility scooter reappeared. He was slaloming in and out of the dashes in the middle of the road and singing, 'For auld lang syne.'

Sheryl put her hand on her brother's shoulder, then on his neck, and they sat there long after the singer had gone and the plane had finally gained altitude and disappeared over the low hills north of the town.

Two hawks

She came into the lounge carrying a blue plastic pharmacy bag. From the bag she took a slim rectangular box. She shook it at him as if preparing the mercury in a thermometer.

'Tonight?' Ray said.

'Tonight,' Karen said.

'Now?'

She nodded and he got up and followed her to the toilet door.

'You're not coming in,' she said.

'No,' he said, 'that sounds right.'

He watched her smiling face narrow and then disappear as she closed the door. At the table he chased the salt shaker after the pepper, then, listening in the direction of the toilet, he made a salt hill. The toilet flushed. He split the hill in two and built the walls of a house. She came into the room.

'What are you making?' she said.

He put his finger through the salt. 'A snow storm,' he said.

'Is it Scotland or Norway that has the blue cross on the

flag?' she said, holding up the thin plastic test. She laughed, but there was a worried set to her mouth.

They stayed up late, talking in the different parts of the house. She came into the toilet while he was there and told him a thing she'd heard from a woman at her work. It's as much to do with the woman's health – plenty have children in their forties. Modern medicine is amazing, he'd said over the sound of his water. They tried some wine, but it didn't fit and they ate a packet of biscuits. We have to consider all the angles, he said. She was sitting on the floor while he lay on the couch, and she went to him and put her hand on his cheek. Two angles, that's all I can see, she said. And later, when they were getting ready for bed she said, You get the pension, *that's* how old we are. He'd held out his hands. Do these look retired? You know what I mean, she said.

The next morning Ray parked his ute and walked around the tree. Two big branches – they were long and thick and there were rip marks where they'd left the trunk – and a lot of smaller stuff had come down. The farmer had sold it as a day's work, which looked about right. Already it was warm and blustery, and Ray was breathing a little when he got back to the truck. He drank from a bottle of water and passed his hand across his face.

There was the paddock with the tree, another paddock containing a small flock of sheep and, abutting that, the farmhouse's back lawn. There were two lambs amongst the flock. They had black socks and black faces and they sprang about and hit their mother's udders.

'Bloody hell,' said Ray, frowning and checking the shape of his chin. As he did a pool toy, caught by the wind, rounded the house and tumbled over the lawn. It was gold with a white belly – shaped like a lion – and it pressed against the fence as if wanting to get out.

. . .

The farm wasn't far from the river where he and Karen had swum on their second date. It was a year ago – the middle of the same hot sort of spring that was more like summer. She'd taken him to an ice-cream shop that turned out to be closed and they'd ended up sitting on a river bank. Ray had been distracted. Their first date had been in an oddly-lit restaurant and there'd been plenty of wine – was she somehow unaware of his age? When she'd suggested a swim he'd blurted, 'Aren't I too old for you?'

'I don't know,' she'd said, getting carefully out of her jeans.

He'd followed her into the black, slow water and gone to where it slithered around his waist. Down river was the bridge they'd used, and he'd watched a truck cross and tried to think of the right way to do things. She'd floated by smiling and then, like an otter, rolled onto her front and disappeared. By the river they'd talked about people they knew – it wasn't a big city and they'd shared a few names. Ray had taught at the university with the father of one of her school friends. It wasn't in question – he *was* old enough to be her father. Then he'd felt her around his knees. She'd swum upstream underwater and hooked on. There were her long arms, her long back and, trailing off her long legs, her long feet. Smiling, he'd widened his base with little steps, then setting his hands on his hips he'd waited for her air to run out.

He'd never stopped worrying about the age thing. There was sometimes a look on her face after they'd made love – she was, he was convinced, imagining a more supple machine. And socially it could be awkward: a night on the couch followed her work do when he'd failed to correct an older woman who'd assumed they were family. But really it was nothing. She'd say things like, This week we're getting

35

right into kissing, or, Wear my legs like a scarf, things that made his heart crank.

He worked with intensity, and by lunch most of it was done. He'd started by using the saw like a filleting knife, sweeping away the whippy outlying branches. Then, as the clouds shaped a nor'-western arc, he'd sawn through the large branches, making sappy rounds – stopping only to clear the sweat, to refuel the machine, to tighten its chain. He'd felt good, and as the sun pricked hot and silver he'd taken off his shirt and then his singlet, and now, as he cut the fuel to the machine and walked back to the truck, the old meat of his hairy belly and arms and shoulders was white with sweet foamy sawdust.

He put his head to one side and then the other and poured water over his hot ears. He sat on the shaded side of the truck and held the meatloaf sandwich in his fist and first the faraway drone of cars on the motorway, then the wind through the tree and finally the sounds of the sheep reached him.

When Ray opened his eyes the lion was flying over his head. It landed, went end over end like a chip packet, and then, seeming to lose interest, stopped and just hovered. 'Excuse me,' said a woman jogging past. She was dressed in two halves: bare feet and old red shorts then a crisp blouse, make-up and jewellery. She came back with the toy stuck under her arm. 'It's the kids' favourite,' she said.

'Likes his freedom does he?' said Ray.

'They use it for tackle practice.' The wind gusted and the lion's rear wagged back and forth chirruping against her arms. She spun the toy expertly and dug around its ears. There was the sound of released pressure and the tightness went out of its skin. She looked up at Ray and said, 'He's under the house.'

'Who?'

'My husband. It's the best place for him.' She smiled brightly as if having made the same joke earlier.

'Men eh?' laughed Ray, holding out his hands.

But she'd finished her joking and wringing the air from the plastic said, 'Piles, you won't get far without good ones.'

In the moment it took to turn from the stack of wood, Ray thought that the voice he'd heard was the farmer's wife's, that she'd returned with something cold from her kitchen. But it wasn't her. It was Karen. In tall black shoes and a black suit, and wielding a thin branch as if it were a wand, she looked straight out of a fairytale.

Fast as summer rain they both started crying.

She dropped her branch and he went to her. She felt as long and cool as a cucumber. 'God etter middag,' she said into his neck.

He held her at the length of his strong arms. She nodded solemnly and said it again. He made his face into a question. 'Norwegian,' she smiled. He laughed and mimicked her. She made her eyes wide and said it as if it were a reprimand. He gave it another go and spit filled the corners of his mouth. She took his big old ears and this time said it with great surprise. He laughed. She laughed. Then they really let go. They held each other's shoulders and bent forward. The wind gusted and they went over like milk cartons, laughing until their wet faces shone like Christmas balls.

Years later Ray and his daughter were standing in front of a tall shallow cave. They'd walked down a long strip of grass that aisled the farmland. There were two pyramid-shaped formations of rock and sandy dunes down to the ocean. They'd been headed back to the car when, at the back of the smaller of the two pyramids, they saw the cave.

'Doesn't smell much like a cave,' said Ray.

'What should it smell like?'

'Animals, old water. Rot,' said Ray. There was a wide shelf in the rock and he sat down. The girl sat down too, and they looked out over the lupins at the blue sky. There was the popping of the broom pods and the smell of hot earth.

'Hawks,' said the girl, pointing.

Two birds, their wings framing the action of their bodies, fell together through the cloudless blue sky.

'Are they fighting?' she said.

Ray squinted and made the sound of a bomb falling and, just before the earth and just before his daughter whooped, the birds parted and went back towards the sun.

The moon

The lift doors open and Peter steps out into the office. His sock is wet from the hole in his shoe. Phones are ringing and people are talking. He walks past his team leader, Bevan, who gives him the thumbs up. Peter sits at his desk and shakes the computer's mouse. The monitor comes on. He pushes his shoe off, puts his headset on, and then enters his password. The big clock on the wall says nine o'clock. He places his cursor on a red phone on the screen and presses a button. The phone turns green and starts blinking. 'Thanks for calling you're speaking with Peter,' he says, watching Tracey, the woman who sits next to him, wave to Bevan as she runs across the office.

At eleven o'clock Peter makes the phone on his screen red. He takes off his headset. His sock is mostly dry and he pulls his shoe on. As he ties the lace it breaks off in his hand. He turns it in his fingers and sniffs at the damp frayed end then puts it in the bin. He shifts forward in his seat and gets up. Melanie, who sits in the pod opposite him, sees him and smiles, then, still smiling, points at her mouthpiece and rotates a finger by her ear.

Peter goes to the lunchroom. He has to curl his toes to stop the shoe coming off. He buys a Coke from the vending machine and sits on a couch. A tall man with glasses and a thin Polynesian man are playing table tennis. The tall man smashes the ball past the Polynesian. It stops in front of Peter who throws it back. 'Thanks,' says the man.

'Not a problem,' says Peter.

At eleven-fourteen Peter pulls himself to the edge of the couch and gets up. When he walks away his shoe stays on the floor. He picks it up. Melanie comes into the lunchroom. 'Hi Peter,' she says, smiling at the shoe in his hand. 'You all right there?'

'Not a problem,' says Peter.

He lifts his foot to get his shoe on and has to hop to keep his balance. His face is red.

'Ooh,' says Melanie. 'Careful.'

He feels her hand on his side. He gets the shoe on and stands up breathing hard. He smiles and says, 'Have a good one.' At the door he looks around. She's putting money into the vending machine. Once, before a team meeting, she sat beside him and asked where he lived and what he did in the weekends. He told her he was part of a karate club and that he went out sometimes. She laughed and made cutting motions with her hands. Her breath smelt like raspberry lifesavers.

Back at his computer he puts his headset on and makes the phone on his screen green. His phone rings.

At twelve-o-nine a female customer asks Peter if he enjoys being an arsehole. In the background Peter can hear a man laugh. The woman asks to speak to a manager. Then she laughs in a hard way and says, 'Do you even know what that is?'

Peter puts her on hold. There's a tight feeling in his stomach. Bevan is drinking from a can and talking to another team leader. Peter rings his extension. Bevan looks down and then over to Peter. He waves his hand and shakes his head. Peter tells the woman someone will call her back. He asks for her phone number. She says the numbers slowly, 'Did you get that, moron?' she says.

In the background the man says, 'Let me talk to him.'

Peter hangs up. He takes his headset off and stands up. Melanie has her back to him. He goes to the toilet. In the cubicle there's a scab of snot on the door. He sits for a while. Someone else comes in. Their shoes squeak on the tiled floor. The urinal flushes noisily and the door closes again. Peter goes to the basin. He tilts his head back, looks into his nose, and then washes his hands. The towel on the dispenser has come free. It hangs down the wall onto the floor. He goes back to his desk.

'Having a good one?' asks Bevan, walking towards him.

'Not a problem,' Peter says, putting his headset on.

'Don't forget my leaving drinks tomorrow night,' Bevan says, bringing his hand to his mouth like he's drinking fast. He pats the back of Peter's chair then goes and stands behind Tracey. She turns around and smiles.

After work, Peter goes to a shoe shop. There are shoelaces under a glass bench. A blonde woman is at the back of the shop. She's using a cloth to wipe a white shoe. The shop smells of leather. Peter looks at the laces and takes some coins out of his pocket. The woman puts the shoe back on the wall and walks over to him. 'Yes?'

'How much are the laces?'

'Seven dollars.'

Peter counts the coins. There isn't enough. 'Oh,' he says. 'Sorry, I left my wallet at home.'

She looks at him for a moment and then walks away.

Peter leaves the shop and walks slowly up the street. In a pub he buys a glass of Coke and goes into a small room filled with pokie machines. There's an elderly woman sitting on a stool in front of a machine. Beside her an Asian couple are whispering to each other. Peter feeds four dollars into a machine and bets one credit a time. He loses the money. He finishes his drink and goes to an ATM to check his balance. 23 cents. He starts back towards his apartment.

Peter was five when his father said to him, 'Your mum's gone to the moon. She has some special work to do. I don't know when she'll be back.'

Five years later Peter was at the mall when he saw her being led by a tall man. She was running her hands across her mouth as if eating a cob of corn. There was another man too. He had skinny legs and was walking fast. Every three or four steps he shook his head and made a parrot sound.

'Look,' said Peter's friend, Simon. 'Loonies.'

Peter started crying.

'Why are you bawling?' said Simon.

Peter covered his face. 'I'm not.'

He looked through his fingers at his mum. Her long hair was now thin and grey. He wanted to go over to her, but he didn't know if she would remember him. She didn't look the same, and the parrot man scared him.

'C'mon,' said Simon.

Peter followed him into a shop. Simon went to the counter and came back with three *Instant Kiwis*. He gave one to Peter. 'If you win you can have half the money.'

Peter scratched the ticket. He got three twenty dollar symbols. He stopped crying.

'Wahoo!' said Simon. 'Let's get milkshakes and more tickets.'

Peter went home when the money was gone. His father was sitting at a table smoking a cigarette and looking at junk mail. He worked at the public library. Sometimes he brought a woman from the library to their flat. 'We're doing a project,' he'd say. 'It's like your one on Ethiopia but more important. That's why L has to stay late.'

'I think I saw Mum in town,' said Peter.

'Who?' There was a bottle of tomato sauce upside down on the table. A fly was crawling over the dried sauce around its neck.

'Mum. She was in the supermarket.'

'Which supermarket?' His father flicked at the fly with the pamphlet. The bottle fell on the floor.

'Centre City. There was a tall man and a skinny man who walked fast.'

'What were you doing there?' The fly was belting against the window.

'I was there with Simon. He bought me a milkshake. People can't live on the moon. Mrs Thompson told us.'

His father went to the window and held the pamphlet over the fly. The fly buzzed. 'So you believe her and not me?' His father put his thumb where the fly was. There was a clicking sound. The buzzing stopped. Peter shook his head. 'Now get off to your room. You won't need dinner if you've been drinking milkshakes,' said his father, looking at where the fly had been squashed.

That night Peter couldn't sleep. He looked out the window at the student flat. Sometimes he saw them being sick into a bush.

His flatmate, Kerry, is in the kitchen.

'Hi Peter, good day?' She takes a jug out of the microwave and pours the contents into a bowl.

'Pretty good,' he says, crossing the small lounge and going into the kitchen. He gets a glass and fills it with water. The smell on his hand reminds him of the pokie machines. He was one penguin away from a hundred dollars.

'Up to anything in the weekend?' Kerry asks, holding

the bowl of noodles and a fork.

Peter shakes his head. 'Just a quiet one.'

'All right then.' Kerry smiles. 'Have a good night.'

He looks at the strands of noodle curling in the sink-hole and hears Kerry on the stairs. He takes a jar of peanut butter and a spoon into his room, sits on the mattress, and turns on a small television. Later in the evening he takes his shirt and trousers off then gets under the blankets. He dreams his mum lives in a hedge.

When he wakes up he eats the rest of the peanut butter, using his finger to clean the sides of the jar. He hears seagulls on the carpark building and thinks of the spinning penguins and polar bears. Kerry comes down the stairs and the shower turns on. At the window he watches cars going into the carpark building. The seagulls and some pigeons are perched on empty concrete flower boxes. He hears high-heeled shoes cross the concrete and thinks of the girl in the shoe shop. Kerry goes back up the stairs. He takes a towel from the back of a chair and goes into the bathroom. At eight-fifty he leaves the apartment and walks to work. By nine o'clock he's at his desk putting on his headset.

The day passes. He is hungry. He drinks thick Milo drinks and eats someone's cheese slices from the fridge in the lunchroom. At lunch he stays at his desk and googles 'International Library'. Bevan comes over. He's wearing a green and black jockey's hat.

'All right Mr Peter? Ready for a drink later?'

Peter nods. 'Not a problem.'

Holding his hands like he's riding a horse Bevan gallops off. When he gets to his desk he turns around and smiles. Beside Peter, Tracey is sipping from a Starbucks cup. She holds a ruler above her head and makes a whipping motion. Bevan bends slightly and, still looking over his shoulder, waggles his arse.

At five-thirty Peter logs off and goes to the lifts. Bevan is looking at a cell-phone and doesn't notice him. Peter rides the lift to the ground floor. Some of his workmates are smoking and laughing on the pavement. They will be waiting for Bevan. Peter goes back past the lifts, through a heavy green door, and into the stairwell. He sits on the bottom stair and waits. After fifteen minutes he checks the pavement. It is empty.

In his apartment he makes a drink out of sugar and milk. He drinks it in his room and then lies down. He goes to sleep. When he wakes up it is dark and his stomach is growling. Kerry and someone else are going past his door. 'Shhhh, be quiet,' she says. 'My flatmate's in there. He's always in there.'

'Oh, okay. Shhhh then,' says a man's voice. There's laughter and feet on the stairs. The door to Kerry's room opens. Peter hears more laughter and the door closing. Outside, on the street, a noisy car changes gears. 'Wahoo!' someone shouts. Upstairs the man coughs. There is quiet and then the sound Kerry makes when she's fucking. Peter gets off his mattress and goes quietly out his door and up the stairs. Her door has a window the size of his television screen. It is partially blocked by a blind. Peter puts his face on an angle and looks into the room. An arse is moving. When it goes down Kerry makes the noise. Peter's cock is hard. The arse speeds up and Kerry makes a longer noise. Peter goes back down the stairs.

In his room he pulls hard on himself then cleans up the spunk with a singlet he keeps under the mattress. Outside someone bellows, 'Yehaa!' Peter straightens the blankets and closes his eyes.

He saw his mum on other occasions: sometimes in a wheelchair, sometimes sitting in the back seat of a van. She always had her hands near her mouth. The last time he saw her, her hair was long and blond, and he thought she must have been getting better. He wondered if she would want to see him, but when he thought about it he realised she was wearing a wig.

In fourth form they studied snakes. There was a video of a python eating a monkey. Then it didn't need to eat for a week. When there was food in the flat Peter thought of the python. During fifth form his father went away for April. 'It's an autumn project. We're doing work on the effects of cold weather on books.' Two years later his father shifted to Timaru.

At the end of his first year of university Peter went to his father's for Christmas. Halfway through the holiday his father told him, 'I've got a job in America. It's with the International Library. You'll have to go back to Dunedin. I don't know when I'll be back.'

From then on Peter stayed in Dunedin during the holidays. He used his student loan to gamble on the poker machines at the pub near his flat. He slept a lot and only just passed his papers. He stopped seeing his mum. After university he applied for the job at the call centre. There was a phone interview and then a job offer. He drew down the last of his student loan and bought bus and ferry tickets to Wellington. Just before Ashburton he saw a man leaning over a fence wearing a red and white hat. He was smoking a cigarette and watching the traffic. It was his father.

In the morning there's a note under his door.

Hi Peter, just wanted to let you know your rent didn't go into my account last night and you still owe me for last month's power. It's no big deal, but I'm not made of money! I'm away tonight but can we sort it out tomorrow? Have a great weekend! K.

Peter looks out the window. The sky is grey. There's a man on a bike going down the road. There are no seagulls, only pigeons. He goes back to his mattress and lies down. He thinks about Kerry and about what she did last night. He gets another hard-on and uses the singlet to clean up the small amount that comes out.

Walking down the street he holds the television in two hands like he's carrying a cake. The man at the second-hand store sniffs when he sees Peter. An unlit cigarette hangs from his mouth while he examines the television. 'Thirty bucks,' he says.

Peter buys a glass of lemonade and feeds the rest of the money into a machine. It has a Wild West theme: squaws, a gold digger, a family on a wagon. He feels good seeing all the credits. The room is empty. 'Okay,' he says.

He loses. There are two dollars left. Lifting himself off the stool he bumps the five credit button. The reels spin: one, two, three, four, five cowboys with golden lassos. The machine whirrs and the credit column climbs up and up. Peter lets out a breath and looks around. He presses CALL ATTENDANT. A light on top of the machine spins. One thousand dollars. Peter sits down. The man who poured his lemonade comes in. 'Nice one,' he says, looking at the screen.

'It was my last spin,' says Peter, watching the man open the front of the machine.

'Uh huh,' says the man, pressing some buttons and writing on a piece of paper. 'I won't be a moment.'

Peter watches the other machines. There is one with pyramids and an Egyptian Queen. He decides to gamble no more than a hundred dollars before he goes back to the apartment.

'Come through,' says the man. Peter follows him into the bar. He has a gold band in one of his ears and he has to move a bar mat to make room for the stacks of money. 'Don't spend it all at once,' he says.

'Not a problem,' says Peter, folding the notes and putting them in his pocket. The door to the pub opens. There is a large figure and rapid feet on the wooden floor. It is Melanie.

'Peter?' she says, smiling. 'You on it already?'

'I was here last night,' he says. 'I left my wallet.'

'Out on the prowl, eh?' There's sweat on her forehead and around her mouth. 'Look,' she says, not letting him answer, 'I'm busting, but you wait right here. Okay?' She looks at him in a serious way and then smiles and walks down the bar. Her big bum rolls from side to side.

The barman is drinking from a white cup. Melanie asks if she can use the toilet. He waves her on. 'Course you can, love,' he says. When she is gone he looks at Peter. 'Your lucky day, pal?' Peter smiles at the man and leans back on the bar. He turns the money over in his pocket thinking of the Egyptians. He could leave and get a plate of chips and a Coke at the pub two doors up. There would be plenty left for Kerry and a new television. But the way Melanie smiled at him and that raspberry smell on her breath? Anyway, it's too late. She's walking towards him. 'So, how are you? It's been so busy at work lately I haven't had a chance to talk. You weren't at Bevan's drinks?' There are pimples on her chin.

'I was out with my brother,' says Peter. 'He's over from Hawaii.'

'Wow, Hawaii? I'd love to go there.' She strokes the air with her hands and arms. 'Hula!' she laughs, and then sighs and touches his shoulder. 'Sorry, I'm a bit loopy today. I think I'm still drunk from last night.' From the back of the pub there are the sounds of a kitchen. The barman has disappeared. His white cup is on the bar. 'I'm off to get a coffee,' she says, pointing at the front of the pub. 'Do you . . .'

'Okay,' Peter says.

When she smiles he can see her red tongue.

. . .

Eight fifty-five, Monday morning. The lift goes up. Peter has heard that if you jump at the right time you lose gravity. He can't remember if you jump when the lift is going up or down. He jumps. The mirrors on the walls vibrate. There is a pain in his foot. He laughs.

He and Melanie kissed. They had been in her bedroom drinking cider and playing Singstar. He'd told her he had a damaged voice box from karate and that he couldn't sing. 'Hai Ya!' she'd said, laughing. 'You tell such funny stories, Peter.' She'd sat beside him on the edge of the bed. He could smell cider and the minty smell of her cigarettes. She told him to wait while she got something.

'Not a problem,' he said.

She came back with a tambourine and picked up the microphone. She sang, 'Waterloo,' in profile, front on, and in profile again. She swayed her arms and shook the tambourine. When she finished she started laughing and had to lie on the floor. Her face was flushed and sweaty and there was a wheezing sound at the back of each breath.

'Do you know about Bevan and Tracey?' she said, puffing on an inhaler

Peter shook his head and drank from the coffee mug. He'd bought the cider and a takeaway pizza after the cafe. When she'd asked about the roll of money he told her about all the money his father was making at the International Library.

'They're shagging.'

Peter looked at her.

'You didn't know? Everyone knows!'

Peter shrugged and drank more cider. He belched quietly.

'Oh, beg your pardon, Mr Burpy,' she said.

She was lying on her side and he could see her stomach sticking below her jersey. It was like his. She pulled the jersey down, rolled onto her stomach, and cupped her face in her hands. 'Come down here,' she said.

'Not a problem,' he said, slipping forward off the end of the bed and sinking onto the soft carpet.

'Lie here,' she said, patting the carpet in front of her.

He put the mug down and went forward onto his hands and then his elbows. He wriggled back so that his feet were under the bed and his face was close to hers. He was breathing hard and her fringe was moving about. She looked at him and smiled. 'Hello,' she said.

'Hi,' he said. He could taste the pizza and hear his heart. He felt her nose on his and there was a little cold air. Then she tipped her head to the side and he felt her lips, and between his lips came her tongue. He put his tongue against hers and moved it. She made a sound. She had her hand on his neck. He moved his tongue again. He liked it. They kissed for a long time on the floor and then got onto the bed where she touched the front of his pants. He lifted up, wanting to feel more of her hand. She laughed and pulled back from his face.

'Not yet,' she said, smiling. 'Let's have some more pizza.'

Peter smiled back at her. This was good.

He sits at his desk and puts his headset on. The clock on the wall says nine o'clock. He makes the red phone go green.

At morning tea he goes to the lunch room. The Polynesian man is by the ping pong table bouncing a ball on a racquet. Peter buys a Coke and sits on the couch. He looks at his new shoes. 'Get ones without laces,' she'd said. 'They're easier to get on and easier to get off.' She'd laughed her husky laugh and put her face into his neck.

'You want to have a hit?' says the Polynesian man. He holds two racquets up like a man on an airport runway.

Peter looks at his watch. Eleven-o-six. 'Sure,' he says. 'Why not?'

Sand

Josh went to the back of the station wagon, opened the boot, and took out his surfboard. Sarah – I'm *essentially* fifteen – was in the back seat. She had headphones on and was swaying so that her long hair brushed side to side over his sports bag and the box of beer. Josh put the surfboard on the lawn. His dad was at the front of the car looking at the bach. There were stairs up to a door that was ajar and, further along, a small broken window. Josh wondered if he could get everything into the bach by himself. Arab and Callum had arrived the day before. The boys' parents had rented the bach as a Christmas present and, though Josh knew his dad wouldn't say anything about the window, he definitely didn't want him to come inside.

Removing the sports bag he managed to snag a bit of Sarah's hair.

'Oww,' she whined, spinning around.

Josh shut the boot before she could say anything else. They had driven over from Hamilton the day before. They had been there for his aunt's fiftieth. Josh couldn't stand it when his dad drank so he'd gone to bed early. In the morning Sarah and his mum were arguing. Sarah had been found with a boy in the back of a Ford Escort.

'A Ford bloody Escort,' their mum shouted.

'Someone must have put date-rape in my drink,' Sarah said. Then she'd picked up her yoga roll and gone out by the hotel's pool.

Beside the bach there was a lawn with a view of the beach and the island. His dad was standing there with his hand shading his eyes. Josh put the bag and the beer next to the surfboard and went onto the lawn. They watched a surfer paddle through a small break. 'It's funny looking at the beach from here,' said his dad, pointing across the water to their holiday home: its huge deck and windows, the trees like giant pineapples.

'Dad, how much does meat cost?'

'Meat?'

'Yeah, to like, barbecue?'

His dad handed him some money. 'Your mum gets rib eye.'

There was a tapping on the window. Sarah was pointing to something in the back of the car. Even if there were no other passengers she never travelled in the front. Their parents complained that they weren't a taxi service, but the one time they tried to force her she'd screamed, 'It's because of what happened to Dan!'

Josh went to the back of the car and looked. She'd removed the blanket he'd put over the bag of grapefruit. 'Don't forget your Vitamin C, Josh,' she said.

As they were leaving that morning his mum had run out to the car carrying the bag of fruit like it was a trophy. She'd stopped smiling when she saw the beer. 'You're encouraging him, John?'

'He'd get it anyway. He's almost eighteen.'

'Seventeen, almost bloody seventeen.'

'They're five minutes away. We'll watch them through the telescope.'

His mum hadn't laughed.

Josh yanked out the bag of fruit.

'Oooh, psycho,' said Sarah, waggling her fingers.

'Enjoy Mum and Dad,' he said, slamming the boot and leaning the fruit against the beer.

'You'll be all right with that?' his dad said, pointing at the gear. 'I don't want to cramp your style.'

Josh nodded. The surfer went down the face of a wave. At a party the previous winter Josh had told a girl about Dan's funeral: about the haka, the Pearl Jam songs, and how they'd buried him with his surfboard.

'It sounds amazing,' she said, and later, in the laundry, she'd let him suck her tits.

'You enjoy this,' his dad said suddenly. He gave Josh a sort of handshake-hug and then walked to the car.

Josh picked up his gear. As he drove off his dad tooted and Sarah stuck her head out the window. *Bye* Joshy.'

He left the fruit and his board by the side of the bach and went up the stairs and inside: stale cigarette smoke. It was the right place. There was a closed door to his right and one in front of him. To his left a doorway and a room. Balled up fish and chip paper, an ashtray, and some loose matches were scattered over a table. He dropped his bag by the front door and carried the beer through. 'Oi,' he said.

Beyond the table was a kitchen and against the walls of the large room there were two single beds. A head and shoulders were sticking out of a sleeping bag. Long grey curtains filled and fell like lungs. The bottles clinked when he put the box on the table. Beside the tomato sauce there was a small pipe. He sniffed its end and then dropped it on the table. He thought about opening a beer. It would look good. Where he stepped there was the gritty crunch of sand.

'Arab?' he said.

Arab didn't move.

'Arab!'

Arab rolled over and opened his eyes. 'Josh,' he said. 'Mate.'

'Where's Callum?' said Josh.

Arab shrugged and rolled back to face the wall. 'Bro, awesome to see you too,' he said.

Josh went back through the doorway. 'Callum you fuck-head!' he said, opening one of the doors. There were no curtains. A tall naked man lay on the bed. It wasn't Callum. Josh shut the door quickly. There'd been a pair of women's underwear on the bed.

'Who the fuck's that in the bedroom?' he said, kicking the side of Arab's bed.

'What?' Arab said.

'In the bedroom? Who is it? It's supposed to be the three of us.'

'That's Si. We met him last night.'

'But . . .'

Arab sat up. His hair had grown even longer and his abs stood out. 'He's got pot,' Arab said, holding his hands as if weighing something. 'He stays, we get pot. He doesn't stay . . .' He sighed. The smell was bad. He lay down. 'He's British, man.'

'Well, what about Callum?' said Josh, going across the room. He waited outside the other door. There was no sound. He knocked and went in. The window above the toilet was broken. A tennis ball was floating in the toilet bowl.

In the lounge Arab was breathing evenly. 'Shit,' Josh said. He drew the grey curtains. The doors to the deck were open. It was warm and still. Below him, on the grass, a pair of board-shorts made a sandy nest for two empty beer bottles. He looked across the water at his parents' place. Two people – Sarah and his dad – were carrying the double kayak down the lawn. When it came to family activities Sarah charged a participation fee.

With the curtains open it was lighter inside. There was a bottle of vodka and a pack of cards in one corner. He picked up a condom box. It was empty except for the lubricant and instructions. He put the lubricant in his pocket and went to his bag where he took out a towel. Outside, beyond the grapefruit and his surfboard, a ten-speed was leaning against the bach. It must have been the pom's. In the seventh form Dan won the school cycling prize. Josh had watched from the back of the auditorium as his brother walked onto the stage. A student yelled something and the other students laughed and cheered. Some of the teachers on the stage smiled. Others thrust their heads forward and narrowed their eyes. Dan shook the rector's hand and everybody clapped. Josh told the boy beside him he was Dan's brother.

'Bullshit,' said the boy.

Josh took the neck of the bike and gave it a shake. It slid down the wall. He went around the bach, down a sand trail and onto the beach. The swell had died. He was happy. He got scared in deep water. Surfing was about being seen with the board. At the beach with his mates he'd say he had a sore arm or that he was too hung-over. Recently, getting his board off a roof rack, he'd pretended to strain his neck.

He sat on the sand and took his T-shirt off. There were only a few hairs on his chest. On his stomach they were sparse and light coloured. Josh walked down to the water. The sand was warm and then it was hard and damp and there was a line of bubbles drying at the high-tide line. In front of the island he could see the on/off flash of the kayakers' red paddles. He went deeper into the water and then forward and under. He kicked just above the bottom. When he looked ahead the ocean was an ominous dark ribbon. He surfaced quickly and stood up facing the beach. Two women were power-walking. Closer to the surf-club, lifesavers were doing things with flags and four-wheeled motorbikes.

Josh lay down by his T-shirt and raked sand up to his chest. He rested his chin on the sand and closed his eyes. After a while he felt the sun burning his back and neck. He turned over and sat up. Dressed in white, an Asian couple were going slowly down the beach. Occasionally the woman would bend over, pick up a shell, and hand it to the man following behind her.

At home in Auckland there was a photo of Dan wearing a pin-stripe suit and carrying a plastic machine gun. His hair was in a pony-tail and the girl with him had a black dot at the corner of her smile. Josh had seen her on Christmas Eve. He, Arab and Callum had been drinking at Callum's brother's apartment in the city. Arab had arrived with some speed, but when they snorted it nothing happened. 'It must be coke,' Arab had said, 'and that takes longer to work.' They'd played drinking games and then gone to a fast-food restaurant. Josh had seen her in the queue and told her who he was.

'He was such a good driver,' she'd said, 'and so good looking.'

Then she told him she was a lawyer and that she was going to London.

'Thanks, about the driving I mean,' Josh said.

She gave him a hug. 'Be strong,' she said, which was something he'd heard a lot around the time of the funeral.

He tried to think of what else he'd have liked to hear about Dan, but in his mind the conversation always ended with her wetting her lips and saying, 'I've got a waterbed at my apartment.'

His hard-on was pressing into his shorts and there was

sand over his chest and stomach. It would look like he'd been playing in it. He sprinted down to the water and went in and under. He stood up and got his hair right. Up at the bach someone was moving across the doorway. The sand was hot and as he ran up the trail he had to stop twice to jump onto his towel.

'Arab, you lazy bastard,' he shouted, going up the back steps.

The tall man was sitting at the dining table. Arab was on the edge of the bed holding an unlit cigarette. They were laughing.

'You missed a fucking huge one last night,' said Arab.

Josh punched him on the arm and took the cigarette. The man at the table stood up. He had short dread-locks and was thin. 'All right mate? I'm Si.' He held out his hand.

Josh slapped rather than shook it. He looked over to Arab. 'Beer?' he ripped open the box on the table.

Arab groaned.

'I'll have one,' said Si.

'Bottle opener?' said Josh, lighting the cigarette.

'You should have bought twist-tops,' said Arab.

Josh went into the kitchen. There was newspaper all over the floor. Some of it was wet and there were chips in the sink. 'Fuck's sake,' he said, going back into the lounge and looking on the table. A *Lonely Planet* had been book-marked with a banana.

'What about a fish slice?' said Si. He had a ring through one of his nipples. It was thick, rubbery, and surrounded by black hair.

'I wasn't going to fry it,' said Josh.

Si went into the kitchen. Josh looked at Arab and shaped his thumbs and forefingers into circles then hung them from his nipples. He made a mincing movement with his hips. Si had a yellow-handled fish slice when he came back. He took

57

one of the bottles, held it a certain way, and back-handed the fish slice up its neck. The lid looped across the room. He had strong forearms and his hand moved fast. The lids popped like they were champagne corks. Arab raised his arm and shouted, 'Ole!' Si put the opened bottles in front of Josh.

'Your sister back from Aussie?' said Arab.

Josh took a bottle and pretended to throw it. Arab flinched.

'You got a sister then?' said Si, filling the pipe.

'He sure does,' said Arab.

Josh held his bottle up and waited for the others to follow. 'To New Year's,' he said.

They all had a turn on the pipe, and then Si went to the shop.

'Yep,' said Arab burping, 'you missed a huge one last night.'

Josh ignored him. He walked onto the deck and called Callum. There was no answer so he left a voicemail: 'Where the fuck are you?' There was a chundering sound from the bathroom. The door was open and Arab was over the toilet. Josh called Callum back. The answer service kicked in and he held the phone next to the column of vomit and shouted, 'Arab says, Happy New Year!'

Back in the lounge, he picked up a beer and the fish slice. The lid came off, but so did a section of the bottle's neck. Arab came in and sat on the bed. Josh showed him the bottle top with the glass still attached, but Arab wasn't interested. He started wiping his chin and mouth with a pillow. 'Oh man,' he said. There was a thundering. It was someone charging up the front stairs. Josh thought of the police and then his mum. The telescope! He was on the deck and starting down the back steps when Si came in with a bag of groceries.

They cooked and ate most of a packet of sausages. Then Arab, who was feeling better after another smoke, trapped a sausage in the fly of his board-shorts and went onto the deck. An old couple were in a car and when they saw Arab they smiled. Arab pretended to ride a horse in slow motion. The woman, who was in the passenger seat, made a flapping gesture at her husband and they drove off. Arab came inside with his arms raised and then pitched the sausage onto a nearby roof. Some seagulls flew down. Si refilled the pipe.

They went to the beach with V bottles filled with beer and sat at the top of a sand dune. There were police in blue shorts and baseball caps and lifeguards in red and yellow dodging toddlers in body-suits and broad hats who ran in and out of the shallows with their arms raised like it was a hold up or a mugging, and everywhere the women wore string bikinis and hotpants and they held bottled water and designer sunglasses and fluoro beach towels and Si and Josh nudged each other and said things about tits and pussy, and Arab rolled cigarettes and told and re-told the story about the old couple and the sausage in the fly of his shorts, and when the sand gently avalanched them to the base of the dune they rampaged down the beach and pelted each other with wet sand and then hit the water like they'd been gunned down and were re-born shouting foul words at the broad blue screen of sky and then dashing back up the beach they flung themselves at the dune where the sand had been fried, no, grilled, where the sand had been in a big fuck-off oven for months, and it made their palms red and shiny and they crawled back to the top and drank hot flat beer and burped and crowed and wrestled and smoked one cigarette after another. Then Sarah came over.

'What are you guys up to?' she said. She was wearing her

favourite white hat – it's seventies fashion, you *so* wouldn't understand – and a red bikini. She had an unlit cigarette.

'We're talking about love,' said Si. He smiled at Sarah and held up his lighter.

Sarah knelt forward to reach the flame.

'We're talking about going out to the island,' said Josh.

'You've been drinking a lot of V,' Sarah said, smiling at Si.

'It's not V,' said Arab.

Sarah put her hand over her mouth as if surprised then tilted her head and exhaled. 'The island?' she said, looking at Josh. 'You'd be scared.'

Arab started laughing then tried to say something, but it came out as a loud hiccough. He pointed at his neck and at Josh. He went onto all fours. He was crying now and the snot coming out his nose was making black cylinders in the sand.

'You're a disgrace,' said Josh.

'The island?' said Si. 'Who's got a boat?'

'You don't need one,' said Josh. 'You just have to get the tide right.'

Si stood and looked. 'See,' Josh said, pointing to where the beach curved and made its closest point to the island.

'Why would we go there?' said Arab.

Si made a cross with his arms over his chest and then pumped his hips with his hands on his arse. 'The Macarena, man!'

The others laughed.

'Can I come?' said Sarah.

'No,' said Josh. 'Boys only.' Then he blushed. But the others didn't notice. They were looking at Sarah.

Arab had left them and gone back to the bach.

'Let's start some proper drinking,' he'd said.

'What, are you scared?' said Josh.

'Nah,' said Arab. 'I thought the idea was to get wasted.'

'C'mon man,' said Si.

Josh clucked and shot his head back and forward.

'What?' said Arab. 'Like you?' Then in a voice that was high and dramatic he said, 'Oh, my poor neck. It's so sore!'

Sarah was talking to some other girls, and Josh thought he and Si had got by without being seen, but then she ran up and held Si by the elbow. 'Si,' she put her hand through her hair, 'can I get some pot?'

'Jesus!' said Josh. He shoved her ahead and walked up beside her.

'That's assault,' Sarah said.

'Get your own friends,' Josh said.

'Is that what you call Arab? A friend?'

'What does that mean?' Josh said.

Sarah looked back at Si.

'Why are you walking like that?' Josh said.

'Why are you walking like that?' she parroted.

The carpark beside the surf-club was full. Towels dried on car bonnets, and people stood around. Tar was melting. A bogan was doing wheelies on a ten speed. Different music was coming from different cars. A rubbish bin was on fire. Two policemen on bicycles were riding towards it. Si had caught up and was walking on the other side of Sarah. She looped her arm through his and tried to do the same with Josh. 'Piss off,' he said.

They drew level with the family bach.

'Dad's getting security guards,' said Sarah. 'He's worried about his trees.' She skipped up the lawn and then stopped and blew a kiss. 'Ciao *boys*,' she said.

The beach narrowed and there were fewer people. Two children with plastic tools were excavating down by the water. Closer to the dunes a man, whose body was a mound of sand, said, 'Nice day for it!'

They walked on.

'I heard there was a riot last year,' said Si.

Josh didn't say anything. He was pissed off. He'd only suggested going to the island to get away from Sarah, but with Si so keen he couldn't back out. Arab was right. They were supposed to be getting wasted.

The sand-bar was almost three hundred metres long and stretched most of the way to the island. Close to halfway there was a submerged area.

'Let's do this,' said Si. The chalky sand squeaked under their feet. A large eyeless fish-head dried in the sun. The sounds of the shore faded. Fishing boats and launches motored up and down a channel on the other side of the island. Long shadowed chutes scarred the island's cliffs. They reached the section of water. It was moving faster than Josh remembered.

'You're sure you've got the tides right?' said Si.

'Yeah,' said Josh. 'I've done this plenty of times.'

Si went in. The water got to his knees then his thighs. Josh watched. If it goes any higher, he thought. But the water was back to Si's knees and, as it got shallower, Si kicked his feet out and ran. Josh started across. There was a nagging weight to the water and he had to walk with his feet close to the bottom. Si had made a long slow turn and zigzagged back; splashing through the water on each side of the bar. His dreadlocks clacked as he hurdled a piece of driftwood and he made another turn in front of Josh who was coming out of the water. They started sprinting. Si was much faster, but Josh felt good. They had beer and pot at the bach. His parents didn't know where he was. They had five full days of it. He held out his hands and made a motorcycle noise. Si looked back and laughed. Sand spat up behind them and they tore towards the island.

There was a seaweedy birdshit smell. Josh sat on a large rock. Si hopped from one rock to another and then started ripping at some mussels. A jetski pulled a 180, making a white spume in front of their bach. The beach was a snake of colour. 'What do you reckon Stuart's doing?' said Si.

'You mean Arab? Maybe he's trying on your underwear.'

Si smiled. 'Let's eat this,' he held up a mussel. He smashed it against the rock and looked inside. He made a face and dropped it then climbed onto a larger rock. 'Could you swim from here?' he said.

'Come on,' said Josh, 'the underwear, whose are they?'

'Hey,' said Si. He was looking down the bar. 'It's your sister.'

'Bollocks,' said Josh, but he climbed onto the rock and looked. It was Sarah. She was entering the section of water. 'Shit,' he said.

She had her arms over her head though the water was only to her knees. She staggered slightly and brought her arms down so they were like wings. Josh thought he could hear her laughing. The water was over her waist now. She staggered again and this time fell. She disappeared. Her foot periscoped and then was gone. The hat was floating out to sea. Josh jumped off the rock and shouted. He started running. Si went past him. Josh tried to go faster. The jetskier had seen them and was idling nearby. His short hair was stuck back from his forehead. Si got to the water and dived forward. Josh jumped the driftwood. He couldn't see her. He ran into the water. The sand was softer and he lost his feet. He was late getting his arms down and the water slapped his face. He came up and looked around. Si was calling out her name and spinning around. Josh went under again and clutched at the bottom. The sand went through his fingers. When he came up again he saw her. She was wiping water off her face and backing onto the beach side of the bar. Si was in the middle of the current watching her. The jetskier revved the machine hard. It leapt forward and into a turn. Sarah raised her hands to the water it laid out and laughed. Then she felt on top of her head and looked around on the sand. Her hat was floating out to sea. She ran out of the water and down the bar. 'Josh,' she shouted, turning and pointing. 'My hat!'

When she walked back her face was sad-looking, but she was doing the thing with her hips and her skin was dark and glistening. Josh got out of the water and stood on the sand opposite his sister. He looked for something to throw.

'I'm piggy in the middle,' Si said. He was still in the water, but closer to the beach side of the bar.

Josh looked at his sister.

'What? It's a free world,' she said, squeezing water out of her ponytail.

'It looks like a goose,' Si said, pointing to where the hat was getting smaller.

But Sarah wasn't listening. She was watching Josh. 'What are you doing?'

He'd made his neck long and was up on his toes. He shivered his body and glared and held his hands out to her. Sarah stopped with her hair when she realised who he was.

'Freak!' she said, wailing and turning and running towards the beach.

Si went out of the water calling her name. He caught her quickly and they stood together for a moment. Sarah spun around. 'I wish it had been you, Josh.' She put her face in her hands. Si rubbed her back. They walked a little way towards the beach and then stopped and Sarah leaned into Si.

Josh sat down. On the lawn in front of his parents' house they were erecting a marquee. Their parents threw a party every year and called it the 'beach hop'. He dug his fingers into the dense sand. It hurt under his fingernails. He was sitting on something. He stood up and felt in his pocket. The lubricant sachet. He ripped it open and squeezed the goo onto his fingers. It was cool and sticky. He dropped the sachet into the shallow hole he'd made and stamped his heel into the sides. Si and Sarah were still standing together. Si shouted and gestured. He ignored them and walked to the ocean side of the bar. There was the white lick of a yacht's sail and further out, where the horizon was hazy, the shape of a ship. Josh looked at his hand. The goo had made a web of his fingers. 'Here I am,' he said, and walked to where the water was submerging the bar. It looked faster and deeper. On the other side Si and Sarah were doing handstands. He flapped his fingers to get the goo off and started to cross.

Maniototo

Mark had been on the dole for three months when he applied for work with an organisation that assisted people with disabilities. There was an interview with two female social workers and Paul. If Mark got the job, Paul was the young man he'd be working with. Paul couldn't talk, so the slim social worker asked the questions on his behalf.

'Paul would like to know what you're doing for work at the moment.'

Mark explained that he'd recently returned from Japan where he'd been an English language teacher. This was true. At fifty he'd been the eldest of the many teachers working for a company that had schools throughout Tokyo.

'Paul, shall we ask him why he left his last job?'

Paul made a short high sound and nodded. Then he stared at his knees for a moment before wheeling back from the desk.

Mark said that he'd been in Japan for twelve months, that his contract had expired and that though he'd loved the country and the teaching he'd been eager to get home. This was not true. He'd been in Japan for eleven months before leaving without telling anyone.

Paul wheeled himself to the other side of the room where there was a pink balloon. There were more questions, most of which Mark answered truthfully. Near the end of the interview Paul came up beside Mark, rested his huge head on Mark's shoulder, and made the sort of sound a man makes at the end of a good meal.

Mark was asked to wait outside. After a while the slim social worker invited him back into the room.

'Congratulations,' she said. 'You've got the job.'

'Great,' said Mark.

'That was easy wasn't it Paul?' said the other woman.

Paul made a new sound. It was long and went up and down and he clapped his big hands together and ran his feet into the wheelchair's foot plates. The two women smiled and started collecting up some papers. Paul stopped his excitement just as suddenly and went back to looking thoughtfully at something on the carpet.

In Tokyo Mark had lived in a small apartment. He slept and ate in one room. There was a window that looked over power lines and the roofs of other apartment buildings. Crows waited on the power lines. There were strict rules on noise levels and disposing of rubbish: if you got the rubbish days mixed up the crows made enough noise and mess for the police to be called.

Mark was terribly lonely for eight months. In the ninth month he decided to start a relationship with one of his young students. In hindsight he blamed the decision on the pressure brought about by living under such a strict bureaucracy and on some chemical in the food or water that had fooled with his brain's architecture.

Dunedin wasn't much better. He hadn't contacted the

67

people he'd known before he left – he'd told them he'd be away for a long time, that after a few years teaching he was going to explore China. 'Just call me Marco Polo,' he remembered saying.

His flatmate in Dunedin was Eric. Eric was saving money so he could mount a court case against ACC. He didn't like to discuss the details of the court case. He spent a lot of time in his bedroom watching television. Once, when Mark heard Eric in the kitchen and went out to talk, Eric went quiet and stood very still next to the washing machine. And he'd stayed that way – like someone pretending to be a lamp post – until Mark left the room.

But now at least, for three hours each Wednesday, Mark saw Paul. The other six days he didn't have anywhere to be so it was a challenge to get up. Sometimes he didn't have time to sort out his long hair or change the T-shirt he'd worn to bed. None of which mattered. Mark was right into freedom, and that definitely included the way a person chose to present themselves.

Having got out of bed, he'd walk to the building where the interview had been held and pick up a car. It was good to be out of the flat, and while he walked he looked forward to seeing Dawn. Dawn was the receptionist. She too was in a wheelchair. When Mark walked in she would smile and, spinning her chair to get the keys off a hook, say, 'Wednesday already? Where does the week go?'

There was something about the way she talked. The occasional word was muffled and as if to make up for the defect she spoke in a loud voice. When she'd finished even a short sentence, her mouth gathered little corners of saliva. She wore blouses. The black one was Mark's favourite. It was stiff looking as if fresh off the rack and she wore it unbuttoned just above her chest. Mark was tall and Dawn was low to the ground. Mark kept eye contact at all times, but it wasn't easy. The skin below Dawn's neck was covered in caramel-coloured freckles.

After seeing her he would drive to Paul's house, which was on the shady side of the city's northern valley. There was a wide path up to a wide front door. Paul shared the house with four other people, and the walls of the hallway were scuffed and marked where wheelchairs had been. Paul's housemates were always out by the time Mark arrived, and the doors to their rooms were closed, sometimes padlocked. One bore the sign, WARREN'S ROOM – NO PARKING, while another featured photographs cut from magazines: a dog in a handbag, Michael Jackson in action on stage.

Going down the hallway, through the kitchen, and into the lounge that was a narrow add-on to the main body of the house, Mark usually found Paul standing in front of the television. Paul didn't use his wheelchair around the house. His balance wasn't great. On open ground with his straight-legged gait and raised arms he resembled a Mummy – after more than a few steps he'd gather speed and then fall. But as long as he had a bench, a wall, or in this case a television to hold onto, he was usually okay. He'd be pointing at the different characters when they appeared on the television screen, while Jax, the woman who ran the house, would be at the dining table in her blue hospital scrubs drinking tea and either disagreeing or agreeing with Paul's taste in cast members. It was a game Paul enjoyed and with every 'Yes' or 'No' he would smack his free hand gleefully against his thigh and huff and puff as if trying to inflate a lilo.

Jax liked dyeing her hair and talking. She cared for Paul and the other people in the house like they were her own children. One time she'd told Mark that the plump social worker had asked her not to wear the scrubs – 'they go against the ethos of our organisation.' Jax said she'd asked what the *ethos* said about changing a grown man's nappies.

And in relating the conversation to Mark, she repeated the words *'grown man'* and made a shape with her hands which suggested something the size of a large mixing bowl.

Paul and his social worker had agreed that Wednesday would be cooking day. The social worker had made him a recipe book. The easy steps of each recipe were shown pictorially: two-minute noodles with chicken, pizza, weiner schnitzel with mashed potato, nachos, and sausages. When Mark asked Paul what he wanted to cook Paul always pointed to sausages. Mark didn't feel it was right to make Paul's decisions for him so each week, after Jax left, they drove to the supermarket and used Paul's money to buy sausages.

Mark's job was to guide Paul through the recipes, along the way teaching him knife skills and the ins and outs of the stove top and oven. But on one of their first Wednesdays Paul put his hand in a hot pan. He bellowed and sat on the floor. When Mark went to help, Paul grabbed his arm and shook him. Mark was thin and Paul was strong. Mark went from one side of the kitchen to the other. This worried Mark. What if something really bad happened? From then on, while Paul sat in the lounge watching television, Mark did the cooking. When lunch was ready they would sit together at the table. Paul ate fast. He could eat three sausages, two eggs and a plate of potatoes during an ad break. It was boring in the house after lunch. There was the television, but Mark watched a lot of television at his flat and he and Paul had different tastes. One day Mark suggested using the time after lunch to go for a drive. Paul agreed.

Mark showed Paul where he'd gone to school and the different flats he'd lived in around the city. Sometimes he talked about women he'd known in the flats, other times he talked about what happened in Japan. 'You've got your whole life in front of you,' he'd say. 'This is valuable information I'm giving you.'

Paul loved music so what he enjoyed most about driving was the radio. As loud as it could go suited him best and he'd shake his legs, clap in time, and if the song was a real beauty he'd pound out the rhythm on the dashboard. Paul and Mark reached a compromise. The first part of the journey was devoted to life coaching while the return journey had more to do with musical expression.

One Wednesday afternoon Paul's social worker called Mark at his flat.

'How was Paul's cooking today?' she said.

'It was good,' said Mark. 'Today Paul cooked Hawaiian pizza.'

'That's awesome!' said the social worker. Then after a pause she asked Mark about the petrol in the work car. She said her boss had gone to use it that afternoon and found the fuel light on.

Mark went red and held the phone away from his ear. He started to think of an excuse.

'You use the car to get from here to Paul's, out to the supermarket and back again,' continued the social worker. 'Remember, Wednesday is Paul's cooking day. That's what he hired you for.'

Mark didn't take Paul driving for a few weeks. They watched television and played the 'Yes/No,' game, but Paul didn't like the way Mark played and he got mad. They tried cooking again, but that first time back, while Mark was peeling a potato, Paul ate most of a raw sausage.

Later, over lunch, Mark wondered aloud whether they should use some of the money in Paul's wallet to buy petrol.

Paul had a full mouth. He looked into his plate and nodded.

Eventually cooking was cancelled. As soon as Jax left, they made for the car. There was a garage they'd stop at for fuel and pies. Then they'd drive. Having run out of life lessons Mark decided to devote the full three hours to musical expression. They passed paddocks of sheep, cows, and kale. They waved to hitchhikers and farmers on tractors. The sea made estuaries and harbours, and long roads wound round rocky coastlines. The car brimmed with positivity. It was helping Mark a great deal. He'd gained perspective on what had happened in Japan and had decided to write to the parents of the student involved. He also planned to write letters to the people who'd employed him – he accepted the need to apologise, but at the same time felt it important that his version of events was recorded.

Other times he thought about Dawn. She'd started wearing bright jewellery and had cut her fringe so it went short to long, mysteriously veiling her left eye. Mark couldn't help but see it as a sign. He decided on a beach ceremony – they'd put down boards to make an aisle and for the first dance he would blow everyone away by taking a turn on the dance floor in a wheelchair of his own.

'You're his new favourite,' Jax said one morning a month after the implementation of the driving policy.

She and Mark were standing in Paul's room. Paul was at the foot of his bed. He'd had a disagreement with one of his housemates and had decided to take time-out in his room.

Mark was looking at a large map that was pinned between the Highlanders' flag and the signed rugby jersey.

'It arrived yesterday –' said Jax.

Paul made his startled sound and the look that went with it.

'You tell him then,' said Jax.

Paul shook his head and looked at his feet.

'Suit yourself,' said Jax. 'It's the –'

Paul sat back with an aggrieved sound. He pointed at the map and then at himself.

'Well then?' said Jax. 'Tell the man, he hasn't got all day.'

Paul took a breath and then, opening and closing his mouth and shifting his head side to side, he made a long, delighted mumbling sound.

'The Maniototo,' said the woman. 'It's where Paul grew up.'

Paul shrieked and clapped and then crossing his arms like an imperious pre-schooler made the mumbling sound again.

It would be their last normal Wednesday. The following week when Mark arrived to pick up the keys Dawn had a new hairstyle and a look on her face. 'Mark,' she said sternly.

'Wow,' smiled Mark, making a motion up from his forehead and giving her new style the thumbs-up.

She looked past him. The slim social worker was there. 'Would you come into my office, Mark,' she said.

Cooking was being phased out. Paul wanted to focus on his weight loss. A student from the Phys Ed School had been hired. Aqua aerobics started next Wednesday morning.

Mark didn't know what to say. 'Next week we're going to do meatballs,' he said.

'I didn't photograph meatballs,' said the social worker.

'It's free cooking,' said Mark.

The social worker shifted some papers on her desk. A chop-sized patch of skin had flushed on her neck. She traced its raised edge with the side of her thumb. 'There are question marks over your suitability for this sort of work.'

There was a sound behind Mark. Dawn was blocking the doorway. Her fringe was gelled straight up as if someone had her by the ankles. Mark shrugged and smiled as if to say, 'What's she talking about?'

Dawn's mouth was as thin and hard as a coin slot on a ticketing machine. She crossed her arms and started to speak.

'Dawn,' said the social worker, making a settle-down motion with her hands.

That afternoon, after their last session, Mark was to return Paul's house key.

Mark stopped in front of Paul's house. The midweek paper drooped wetly from the mailbox. One thrush followed another across the wide path. A balled-up nappy was lodged in the thin hedge. Mark rested his head on the steering wheel. The fluorescent shoes he'd bought on his first day in Tokyo looked as frayed and colourless as a fish run through a washing machine. He sat back and moaned. He was supposed to be in Shanghai.

There was a clattering out on the road. It was the postie. He had a sleeveless post office-red polo shirt, tattooed thighs and a moustache. He was up on the pedals and going for it. There was a puddle on the footpath and he made a bunny-hop: the pannier bags lifted and the big wheels turned up a spray. He spotted Mark and, steering with one hand and sitting as if on a tall horse, he made a decisive salute.

There was something over Mark's scalp and down his spine, something deep in his balls that made him square his shoulders and tilt his jaw, and, as he turned in his seat and watched the postie make a diagonal charge across the road, it came to him – the Maniototo: he would take Paul home.

Inside the petrol station, the attendant – he was a small man with a horseman's walk – took the money at the till and said, 'Twenty? Going a bit further today?'

'The Maniototo,' said Mark.

The attendant told Mark he knew the Maniototo like it

was the back of his hand. Then he told him about the Old Dunstan Road. 'Fastest way in is through Clarke's Junction. It's the trail the miners made during the gold rush. Not that you'd go in what you're driving. You'd want something with a bit more tit.'

But Mark had stopped listening. He was gazing out over the forecourt to the car, where Paul, his hands resting patiently on the dashboard, was waiting for the music to re-start.

Ten kilometres out of Clarke's Junction the radio went from Classic Hits to static and the road that becomes the Dunstan trail went from asphalt to gravel. Paul too changed. Instead of enjoying the landscape — a vast slope of tussock — he folded in at the shoulders and stared into his lap.

Leaving Dunedin he and Mark had really turned it on. 'I'm taking you back to your land,' Mark had shouted over the music, and then during the next song, as Paul was working up a blistering rhythm, he'd hollered, 'Manioooooooototoooooo,' and Paul's face had gone red and then crimson and he'd pummelled the dashboard, the door frame, and the ceiling.

'Your land,' said Mark, pointing out the windscreen.

Paul shook his head.

'This is where your spirit resides,' said Mark.

Paul pointed into his mouth and made the dry sound the plughole makes when the last of the water's drained.

Revelling in Paul's mighty percussion Mark had been sure of it all. Dawn, the social workers, the aerobics instructors, they had no idea. This path, he'd thought, is the path to humanity. But now there was a gap in the fences and a cattle-stop. He piloted them across, but though he smiled at Paul, as if the shuddering were all part of the plan, Paul didn't look up or do anything. After the cattle-stop the trail became two steep lines of dirt. Mark revved the car and changed gears and a cow that had been watching turned and went lazily into the tussock.

In half an hour they were atop the first of a corrugation of four ranges. To the west, far beneath them, was the Great Mossy Swamp, and all the way to its shore strange croppings of rock – like melting shrines – marked the tussock. The steering wheel had started to rattle and there was a new draft through the floor of the car. Paul – he'd long since stopped responding to the normal prompts in the normal way – sat looking into his lap.

Mark drove on. The look he'd adopted after the postman's tribute had slackened. In the waning autumn light, his features modelled a life of wrong moves. There was a gentle curve in the road and then a puddle the size of a paddling pool. The puddle turned out to be deeper than it looked. The car went in and stopped. Mark changed gears and rode the engine. He shook his thin body forward and then back. Water splattered the back window. He put the car into reverse and trod hard on the accelerator. There was a sound like a courgette being snapped. He reached down. The accelerator pedal was now no longer part of the car. The puddle was coming through the floor. 'Um,' he said, 'I might try and give us a wee push.'

Paul shifted his hands in his lap, but didn't say anything. Mark got out and went to the back of the car. It was cold. The land appeared as something turned upside down, or like something you'd expect to see through the porthole of a submarine. He set his feet wide and pushed. It was like pushing at a shipping container. He went to the front of the car and looked through the windscreen. He gaped at Paul and made his hands into ears. On a shot-up sign a hawk flapped its wings and rose into the sky. Paul didn't stir. Mark got back into the car and looking over at Paul, nodded as if they were in a restaurant and he'd just returned from a satisfactory visit to the rest room, then he sat and watched the icy night drain into the day.

★

One hundred and forty years earlier the miners spent their nights in shacks, tents, or nestled into the tussock. They travelled alone or in small groups, and, depending on the ravel of the man's brain, he thought of the cold, of food, of the smell off his woman's neck and of course of gold nuggets: sized like an axe head, a dinner plate, a newborn babe.

Orderly

The patient had refused to travel by bed so Dale had her in a wheelchair.

'I'm not so sick that I need to go in a bed. And anyway,' she'd said, 'you look too old to get me *and* a bed moving.'

On any new orderly's first day, Lane, their boss, would tell the same joke: 'The patient's always right,' then working his neck side to side he'd say, 'except when I'm around.'

Dale had been at the hospital for one year. He'd already heard the joke plenty of times.

'What's your surname?' said the woman in the wheelchair.

'Harper.'

'And what was it before your civil union?' The woman made a neighing sound that turned into a wheeze.

Dale didn't say anything. She was heavy. Going out of the ward one of the chair's wheels got stuck. He crouched – there was a bad smell from her hair – and pushed with his legs. At the lifts he pressed the down arrow and waited. The lift came. He backed the chair on, pressed the button for the Lower Ground floor, leaned forward with his hands on the handles and watched the numbers above the doors light in descending order. The lift stopped. 'Here we are,' he said. The four lifts opened onto a wide passageway that joined the emergency department to the oncology unit. The radiology department was in between. As Dale pushed the woman towards the department's waiting-bay he handed Lily, the receptionist, the woman's x-ray request slip.

'Shouldn't be too long.' Dale said, parking the woman next to a young man in a bed. Half his body was in plaster and his leg was suspended by wires attached to the frame of the bed.

The woman in the chair peered at the young man. 'What's your surname?' she said.

Dale went past the reception and down a corridor. There was a staffroom halfway down the corridor and at the end, backing onto the x-ray suites, a large room where the radiographers worked. Off that room was the orderlies' office. Lane's desk was at one end. Jobs came in from all the different wards and Lane entered them on the computer before distributing them amongst the orderlies.

There were three chairs down each wall. Dale sat down. They were forbidden to rest their feet on the chairs opposite.

Lane was just finishing a call. He liked to talk about hunting, specifically the part where the animal dies. Sometimes he'd demonstrate the exercises he performed in his home gym. 'Coffee,' he said, writing the next job on a piece of paper.

'Eh?' said Dale, sitting forward.

'I always have a strong cup before bed.' Lane smiled and put the piece of paper on the desk.

'Coffee, eh?' Dale patted at the hair on the top of his head. He wore it longer these days. With a bit of inventive combing it looked like a full head. 'Wouldn't the caffeine keep you awake, Lane?'

Lane smiled and tapped his nose. 'You're not listening,

Dale. I didn't say bed, I said *bed*.'

'Oh righto,' said Dale, smiling and leaning forward to take the piece of paper. But Lane was faster and he stretched forward and held it up like it was an ace.

'I don't drink it every night,' Lane said, 'only when Marlene's over.' He leaned back and put his hands behind his head. He stared at Dale with his black eyes.

Loren came in. She was slow. She'd been an orderly for so long that even when she wasn't pushing a bed or a wheelchair she walked with her forearms at ninety degrees. Only she and Feroz had been radiology orderlies for longer than Dale.

'So, coffee might be just what you need, Dale,' said Lane, handing him the paper.

'Coffee?' said Loren. 'No.' She shook her head as if trying to shake the words free. 'I drink Milo.'

Dale glanced at the paper and put it in his pocket.

'The All Blacks drink Milo,' said Loren.

'Yeah, righto Lorry,' said Dale. 'The All Blacks eh?' He stood up and drew his hands back like he had a rugby ball and was about to make a lineout throw.

Loren reared back as if he had an axe. 'Assault,' she shouted. 'Assault in my workplace.'

'Dale, get off and do that job,' said Lane, and then, 'Calm down Lorry, he couldn't bring down an ant.'

Dale went out of the office, around a cluster of radiographers, and down the corridor. Instead of going right and past reception he went left and past the bean counters' offices, past the specialised x-ray studios, the staff toilets, the changing rooms, the spare wheelchairs and the bags of linen. In the stairwell the loose skin above and between his eyes creased causing his eyebrows to stand up and for a moment his face almost looked predatory. 'Coffee?' he said, and then in a rhythm which matched his each descending step, 'Can't a man be left to get on with his own bloody job?' He shoved through the swing doors that led to the back corridor of the CT and Ultrasound departments. The walls were long, dimly lit, and scuffed and dented by beds. His shoes squeaked on the linoleum, a machine whirred in a vacant surgical suite, and in an alcove a heap of dirty scrubs made the shadow of a wolf on the wall.

Outside the two CT rooms there was a Polynesian woman on a bed. Under the bed a small brown boy was holding a book with a goat on the cover. The woman was crying and had one arm around her stomach. Her other arm hung down the side of the bed and she was beckoning with her hand and talking, between moans, in the tone you would use to call a pet. Dale took the paper out of his pocket.

'Mrs Edwards?' he said, looking at the woman.

She pointed under the bed and said something Dale didn't understand.

'English, you speak the English?' asked Dale, looking at her wrists and on her bed for notes or a name tag. There was nothing. A nurse in blue scrubs was coming. Her grey hair was in a bun and as she walked the loose strands rode the breeze. Dale knew the nurse. She belonged to a bowling club not far from his flat. 'Cheap beer and lots of men,' she'd say. He always forgot her name.

'Hi Dale,' she said.

'Is this a Mrs Edwards?'

The nurse shrugged as she went past. 'Not my patient. Ask someone in there.' She pointed at the control rooms.

Dale looked back at the woman who was still gesturing under the bed. He got down like he was checking a tyre. The boy was eating something off the floor. 'You don't want to be doing that,' Dale said. He reached out and took the boy's foot, then he made a face and shook out his tongue. The boy laughed. Dale took the other foot and shook his tongue some more. The boy laughed again. Dale pulled, gently sliding the boy out on his bum. 'There we are,' he said, picking him up and giving him to the woman. She held the boy close and gave him a strand of her hair to suck. The book was still under the bed and Dale retrieved that as well. Dale showed the book to the woman. 'Goat,' he said, making horns of his hands. The woman smiled and patted the child's bottom. Dale slid the book under a pillow and said the word again. He bleated and made a butting motion. The woman said something and laughed. 'There we are,' said Dale.

A linen trolley clattered out by the lifts. Dale remembered himself and went briskly into the control room. On each wall, along with the computers and boards of dials and buttons, two windows looked over the massive mechanical sleeves. 'Hello?' said Dale, but the rooms were empty. He stood in front of the computers and raised his finger like he was testing the wind. 'Houston, we have a problem,' he said, staring at a large red button.

There were footsteps and just before them the wind people bring underground. Dale thrust his finger into his ear and turned. There was a young Indian woman in a white coat. The Queen, that's what Feroz called her. Feroz was Fijian-Indian and when he told a story or joke about her it would be: 'Dale man, you're not going to believe what the Queen said.' His head would bobble and he'd put his arm around Dale's shoulder and, at the end, if it was a really funny story, he'd slap Dale's stomach or even clutch his knees.

'Mrs Edwards?' asked Dale, putting his hands in his pockets.

'No,' said the doctor. She was holding a book of notes. 'I'm about to scan Mrs Tapisi.'

'Tapisi?' Dale took out the piece of paper. 'This says Edwards.'

She grabbed the paper. 'You bring this patient to us,'

she shook the paper in his face. 'Mrs Edwards *from* 7D. I'm scanning her next.'

She was right. Lane's coffee story had distracted him. 'Thanks,' Dale said, taking the paper. He heard her laugh behind him.

'Where do they find you people?' she said.

You people. The woman with the child smiled at him as he went past her bed. 'Don't worry about me,' he shouted, waving like he was dusting a black board. 'This place'll do your ruddy head in.'

He stomped around to the lifts and pressed the button. Lane would have him on the stopwatch. There'd be hell to pay. The lift came and he got on. It stopped on the third floor and two specialists took their time getting on. Dale leaned against the back wall sneering at them. Dressed up like bloody golfers. The doctors murmured to each other, and the lift went slowly upwards, shuddering as the giant pulleys groaned and whined. Sometimes a lift broke down, and men in grey overalls went up through the man-holes and clattered around with wrenches and spanners. 'One of these days something's going to come completely unstuck around here.' The doctors looked at Dale. One of them started to say something, but the lift doors opened onto the seventh floor and, wearing his predator's face, Dale marched between them.

A man was asleep in a wheelchair in the corridor. The back of his head was resting on the bottom of a fire extinguisher. Two nurses, big thighs rolling under blue smocks, went past. They didn't look at Dale. 'Bloody fire hazard!' he said, thumping the wall. The sleeping man woke up. His Adam's apple pumped forward and then back. Dale glared at the list of names on the whiteboard outside the first room of the ward. He shook his head and kept walking.

A linen trolley, its chipped blue ribs containing logs of

linen bags, was coming. Salu was pushing it with one arm and sucking noisily on his teeth. 'Hey Dale, my man,' he said. His hair was cut high over his ears.

'Can't stop, Salu,' said Dale, shaking his head. But then he did stop and, sighing to finally let out a breath, he turned around and said, 'What's on the lunch board today, Salu?'

They always talked about the menu at the staff cafe: meatloaf, shepherd's pie, spaghetti bolognaise, hamburgers, the Friday surprise. But Salu was busy. Steering the man in the wheelchair out of the way with one hand and towing the linen trolley with the other. Good old Salu. Dale strode to the nurses' station. 'Hello Mary,' he said.

'Who you after, Dale?' Mary said. Her fingers were so bony it looked like a gentle pull would joint the lot.

'Edwards, for CT –'

'A Ms, in room three.'

'Thanks Mary,' said Dale. He went into the room. 'Taxi for Ms Edwards,' he said.

That winter the hospital was sixty. The sealant around its windows was failing and the drafts were murder. Curtains to be drawn at all times. Lights blazed and surfaces shone.

'Paging Ms Edwards?'

'Down here. That one,' said a legless plump woman.

There were six beds in the room. The plump woman was in the bed at the far corner and she was pointing to the bed opposite hers. The old woman there was bent like a staple, bent so far forward that from the end of her bed, and beneath her hospital gown, Dale could see the length of her spine. 'A young lady for CT?' he said, going to the head of the bed and knocking on a bedside table.

'She's not young,' said the plump woman. In a red satin slip she looked like some sort of circus balloon.

Dale pulled the bed-curtain across. A strand of drool joined the old woman's mouth to the sheet. He hooked his arm under her armpit and settled her back then chocked her with pillows and spread the covers up her front. With tissues from the bedside table he cleared her nose and while he worked he told her who he was and where they were going, but she just looked through him as if he were a window and, as if through the window, she could see someone coming, someone she'd been looking forward to seeing for an awfully long time.

Dale flung the curtain back and unlocked the bed's wheels with the toe of his shoe. He checked once again she wasn't attached to a drip or a blood bag and that her catheter bag was properly fastened. Finally, he turned her wrist to re-check the name on her wrist-band. 'Haven't you got your own watch,' she said, in a firm and loud voice, but then just as quickly she returned to her stupor, not staring, but tilting forward so that despite Dale's work with the pillows, her forehead sunk back to the covers.

'Ropes away,' cried Dale, bringing the bed out from the wall in a smooth motion and walking backwards with it down the middle of the room and into the corridor. A nurse was waiting with a folder of notes.

'Off for your CT, Ms Edwards?' she shouted, patting the woman on her hand and putting the folder on the bed. 'We'll get you a nice cup of tea when you come back.'

Dale brought the bed into line and then gave it another tug. He dodged with matadorian flourish and let it glide by straight and true. For a moment he walked alongside as if it were nothing to do with him and then caught its head and coached it past the man in the wheelchair. 'You directing traffic?' said Dale.

The man smiled broadly and signalling frantically in both directions caused the fly of his pyjamas to spread and expose a withered-looking handful of plumbing. 'Eyes left Ms Edwards,' commanded Dale, leaving the ward and arcing through two elegant turns to park in front of the transport-lift. He went around the bed and picked up the lift-phone. It rang once.

'Yep?'

'I'm on seven.'

'Yep.'

The lift came and the doors opened. It was Sione. He was dressed the same as Salu. The linen orderlies took turns manning the lift. Sione wore an earring and a moustache. He smiled at Dale, reached out a huge hand, and grabbed the end of the bed, pulling it straight into the lift and stopping it just as suddenly. Ms Edwards rocked forward and then back petting the covers with her forehead.

'Where to Dale?'

'Basement please.'

The doors closed and the lift thunked and shuddered before starting.

'You hear the one about the man and the chicken?' said Sione.

Dale shook his head. As soon as he'd stopped moving he'd started worrying. It had been twenty minutes already. Lane was going to string him up.

'I'll tell you when there isn't a *lady* present,' said Sione, looking at Ms Edwards who didn't move or say anything.

The doors opened onto the basement. Dale pulled the bed out of the lift and brought it around. 'Hey Sione,' he said, 'can you wait a minute and take me to LG?'

Sione nodded and leaned into the back corner of the lift. And as the air conditioning pipes in the ceiling made their strange hoovering sound Dale pushed hard for the doorway to the CT corridor and then started his turn. Like a speedway pro, he used the sideways momentum of the bed to take it into the tight corner and, just as the bed seemed sure to smash into the door frame, and as Ms Edwards resurfaced and made the sound of a child on a slide, Dale powered up his old legs and came at a canter out of the corner.

'Safe as houses,' he said, docking the bed, scooping up Ms Edwards' notes, and hurrying into the room with its lights and computers. 'Ms Edwards,' he announced, putting the notes on a desk and jogging back to the lifts.

'A man arrives home with a live chicken under his arm. His wife's watching the TV and the man says, "So, this is the pig I've been fucking."

'"That's not a pig," says his wife, '"that's a chicken."

'"I wasn't talking to you," says the man.'

The lift doors opened onto LG. Dale went out smiling. Behind him there was silence as Sione took a breath and then a great gust of laughter. Dale turned around. Sione was coming out of the lift with his arms out like he was wrestling a bear. The phone rang and, still laughing, Sione went back and answered. As the lift doors closed he saluted. Dale smiled some more and then the chicken clicked into place with the pig. First his thin shoulders went and then the muscles between his ribs caught. He was still laughing as he went past Lily, but with each step down the corridor the warmth inside him grew cold. He went into the office with his hands in a monkey-grip around each wrist.

'Glad you could join us,' said Lane, undoing his top button. 'Would you close the door, Dale?'

You knew it was bad when Lane smiled. Dale closed the door. He could hear people out by the lifts and he wondered if Lane had heard Sione's joke. When he turned back Lane had his shirt undone. He was wearing a singlet. Lane kept the deodorant beside the photo of the dead animal on his desk. Dale looked down at his hands then put them on his hips and then behind his back. He heard the bottle shake, the smell of it, the progress of the perfumed ball.

When Lane had finished his toileting he buttoned his

87

shirt and sat back with his hands behind his head. 'So?' he said. The computer hummed and the incoming call light on the phone flashed.

Dale stepped from one foot to the other. 'Instead of going to 7D to get my patient I went to CT.'

'I know that,' said Lane. 'I've just been talking to CT. They said you were mucking around down there. The nice doctor thought you should get your eyes checked.'

'I should have read your note more closely.'

'20/20 vision,' said Lane, holding his thumb and forefinger up to his eyes. 'I see deer before they see me.' He showed the photo like it was identification.

Dale went over to the desk and looked. Lane squatting with a rifle and a dead deer. He'd seen it a million times. 'Righto,' he said. He went to sit down.

'Uh uh,' Lane said. 'Stay where you are.' He opened a drawer and took out a piece of paper. 'We've been down this track before haven't we? Time wasting on: the twenty-first of July, the seventh of September, the ninth of April. Today being,' Lane looked at his watch, 'Dale Harper, today being the ninth of November, I am giving you your first verbal warning for malingering.' Lane sat forward in a pleased way and wrote on the paper.

'But,' said Dale, 'I was helping an old lady on the seventh floor, and there were the Islanders in the basement.'

'Islanders?' said Lane, coming up from his seat and around the front of his desk.

'He was under the bed with a book. There was a goat.'

Lane was shaking his head. 'Dale, Dale, Dale. We don't call them that anymore.' He sat on the front of the desk. 'Polynesians,' he whispered.

Dale didn't know what to say.

'I don't want to have to bring more serious action against you, Dale, but that seems to be where this is headed.' Lane stood up from the desk. They were around the same height though Lane was much broader. Dale could feel Lane's breath against his face. He wanted to step back, or to do something.

'Now, I've got a job for you Dale.' Lane took a red square of paper from the desk. Someone knocked on the door.

'Lane?' It was Feroz.

'Wait out there,' said Lane. He held the paper up. 'Read this to me, Dale.'

'Lange 6b to X-Ray. On a chair.'

'And what does that mean?'

There was another knock on the door.

'Hold on, Feroz,' shouted Lane. It was like a foghorn.

'Bring patient Lange down from 6B on a wheelchair,' said Dale.

Lane took two short steps and stood on Dale's toes. At the same time he grabbed Dale's shoulders. Then Lane kissed Dale. Dale felt the jamming of his feet and Lane's hands, they were like lead gloves, but mostly it was Lane's breath, Lane's nose squishing into his, and the flinty press of Lane's teeth. There was a sound, a high closed off pant, and it was over. Then Lane was no longer in front of him, but was opening the door.

Feroz came in. 'You and Lane in a secret meeting, Dale?'

Dale looked at Feroz.

'Hey Dale, you okay, man?'

Lane said something, but Dale was leaving the office: rounding a huddle of radiographers, passing the staffroom and going through a family of Asians who were clustered around the reception desk. A lift was waiting, doors ajar. He went inside and pressed the button for the sixth floor. The lift started upwards. He stood on one side and then the other. There was a chip packet stuffed between the wall of the lift and the hand-rail. Prodded, it fluttered scratchily to the floor. He saw and then felt Lane's dry lips. Lane's thin, dry lips.

Entering the ward Dale held the red paper in two hands like it was a steering wheel or a shield. He was trembling. With no Lange on the whiteboard outside the first room, he went further into the ward and scrutinised the board on the wall outside the next room, but that too was no good. Two nurses were standing beside a water cooler. On a plate on top of the cooler were the remains of a chocolate cake. 'Chocolate cake,' said Dale breezily. 'Feroz likes his chocolate cake.'

They looked at him with bland expressions. One of the nurses had a box of cigarettes. She opened and closed the lid.

'Somebody's birthday, eh?' Dale said.

The nurse with the cigarettes turned back to the other nurse.

Dale rubbed at his mouth and, not bothering to check the board, went into room three. There were two old men in beds, and a trolley of piss bottles. Opposite the beds, already in a wheelchair, and with a folder in his lap – the word Lange in black felt down its spine – was a huge man: grey skin, giant glasses, and a brown dressing gown. 'Good to go,' said Dale, more to himself than Mr Lange.

When Dale got out of the ward, the lift he'd ridden up was waiting, doors ajar. He backed on and pressed the button for the lower-ground floor, but nothing happened. He jabbed the button with his forefinger. The doors fluttered for a moment and then closed reluctantly as if resisted by a strong body. He gripped the handles and tried to concentrate on the light in the numbers above the doors. Five, four, but no three, just a strangely gentle tearing sound. Then the lift stopped.

★

Before his death, Mr Lange would describe the hour he spent in that broken down lift as one of his strangest. There was the initial outburst as his orderly slammed from wall to door like a blow fly in a shoebox: 'I told them. I bloody told them!' Then the second round, and this was when Mr Lange had to use his firmest language, when the orderly climbed the back of the wheelchair and attempted to clamber through the manhole in the ceiling of the lift: 'I'll only come out at night!' After that, and to Mr Lange's great relief, the man faded somewhat. Mr Lange was still facing the lift doors and, hearing the man weeping and muttering, he managed, with some considerable effort, to reverse and turn his wheelchair.

The man was folded into the corner of the lift gripping his wrists. Mr Lange tentatively offered a question around claustrophobia and when the man shook his head he started on a more general line around the man's hobbies (they shared an interest in rugby league) and most relevantly, his working life at the hospital.

If that hour in the lift was a peculiar one for Mr Lange, the hour following the entrapment was merrily described as the last truly satisfying work of his life. When he recalled that time in the narrow office (in order to fit his wheelchair the orderly removed the six chairs with the solemnity of a bailiff) his tired yellow eyes blazed, his once voluminous voice rediscovered its grandeur, and he was able to announce with the great surety of the dying that the truism (about hunters and the hunted) had once again shown him the sweet barb of its tail.

People's homes

My son Tom was three when I started as a fairy. Vern had just left us, and I took a job doing children's parties. I was one of three fairies. Our boss owned a shop called Pinky's Party Store, and we would meet there on Saturday mornings to load our cars and get changed. The other two were younger. They went to drama school and were always talking about new ways to *engage* the children. But I took the job because it was weekends only when a neighbour could look after Tom. After a certain amount of fairying I started stealing from the houses where I performed.

All Vern left us was his shoe, and after a few days crying I remember screaming and throwing it through our bedroom window. I went out to where it was and returned it through another window. Then I heard Tom howling. I found him under the table with his hands over his ears. His skin was the same colour as the side of a bath. Vern and I had taught him that if there was an earthquake – wobbling, cracking, crashing – he was to get under that table. The shoe was nearby and before picking him up I put it in the fire. And as I held him and we both cried I made the previous four years into a spider and sealed it in a preserving jar. The jar went far back in a high unused cupboard and from then on I only saw Vern when I slept.

I rented a one-bedroom unit on the cold flat land between the head of the harbour and the sea. I sold the furniture that wouldn't fit and signed up for the benefit. It was winter. We had the heater going all the time. Mould came through the walls and Tom spent time on oxygen in the hospital. If we wanted to be comfortable and well-fed I needed a job. That's when I started at Pinky's.

The props filled the car. The pink secret staircase jutted from the boot like a huge tongue. With the star out the window, the giant wand just fitted in the back seat. Its opposite end was a sharp spike and the first thing I did when arriving at a party was plant it in the front lawn. The magic blanket was under the wand and it too was pink and shiny. There were mandarin-coloured tassles down each edge and the children had to sit on it with their arms and legs crossed if they wanted to go on adventures. There were complimentary wands and wings in the passenger seat's footwell and fizz and dessert food filling the seat itself. A certain type of parent covered the carpets and sometimes the furniture in a layer of clear plastic. I was always wary stealing from those houses.

The first thing I stole was a batch of sausage rolls. They were on a bench with a lot of other food and with nowhere better to hide them I rolled them into the magic blanket. I had time before my next booking so I parked the car overlooking the beach, got into the back seat, and retrieved the pastries. They were squashed and there were bits of fabric and god-knows-what stuck to their oily skin, but I ate what I could and bagged the rest for Tom. I gave the blanket a good shake and then watched from the car as the seagulls fought over the scabs.

After loading the car I would get changed. There was a pink wig, wings sewn to a pink vest, bracelets around my wrists and upper arms, tights, a lavender tutu, and ballet shoes. The mask was optional. I tried it once but breathing was hard and one of the children went off screaming. After that I stuck to make-up and, following the theft of the sausage rolls, I stole from almost every house I went to. Among other items there were pot plants, a school bag, a frying pan, a carving set – and from the same house a frozen chicken.

My show excluded adults. The men especially liked to hang around. They would hover in doorways or sometimes sit like museum exhibits in the rooms where I was to perform. But they never stayed long. I had a special look for them. I imagined they were Vern. If they were respectful I took less. If they leered or sneered I took more. But only what I needed and could get easily: one smooth movement, there and then gone. One time, though, was different.

It was my last booking of the day. I'd already stolen a bag of green apples and a hand-held blender. Tom was back in hospital. He'd come off a swing and broken his jaw. The doctor had said to feed him pulp. I found the house and as usual sank the giant wand into the front lawn. Faces and hands pressed against the windows and then the door opened. They came like schooling fish: around the wand, over to my car and the pink staircase, and around and around me as I carried the magic blanket into the house and whispered to them not to touch its tassles.

'They're covered in travelling dust. You do want to see the Monkey Princess?'

I unpacked the rest of my gear then we darkened the lounge and boarded the blanket. Not long after take-off, over the ocean just before Monkey Land, a curly-haired boy tumbled off. His face convinced them he was falling towards the polar bears and their black scissor teeth. There was hysteria. But Fairy Daisy got quickly into position and retrieved the boy with her magic hand of hope. It was a safe journey after that. We sang a waiata to the Princess and played upside down racing with the silly blue baboon gang before going out to the wand.

I'd just finished packing when a woman I hadn't seen before came out to the car. She was holding a cheque and a glass of wine.

'Thank you,' she said. 'My Robert particularly enjoyed the race to nowhere.'

Every few words her lips closed and her throat worked up and down as if there were bubbles coming from her stomach. She was drunk. 'You must find it exhausting,' she said.

Before each party I imagined myself and the children surrounding a paddling pool. We detached a part of our skulls then strong hands held the bum of our trousers and tipped us like gravy boats. Our brains plopped into the pool. There was hacking and mincing and then communal brain meat for us all.

'I feed off the children.'

I'd left a bucket in the hallway. But she wanted to talk.

'When *we* were young there was pass the parcel.' She was leaning near the back window of the car and swaying so the wand's star sometimes covered her face. 'Occasionally there were balloons,' she said, looking up at the sky. From the house there was a blast of party music, quiet, and then a child's howl. 'My bloody brother,' she said.

The wine in her glass was thick and yellow-looking and she took a deep draught. I'd stolen vitamins once. The morning after Tom had screamed from the toilet. 'Mummy!' Neon yellow piss arced around the bathroom. Afterwards he'd told me he thought his penis would be too hot to touch.

'We've got balloons at the store,' I said.

'Of course one does have to be careful.'

I went up and down on my toes and then smiled at her. 'I just want to check I have everything.' I pointed back at the house.

'All the mothers think you're beautiful,' she said, squeezing at the point of the star like she was testing fruit.

I started across the lawn.

'I suppose the fathers think the same,' she said.

The front of the house was quiet. There were high ceilings, a staircase, and a painting of a street under snow. We'd played disco giants up and down the wide hallway. The door to the lounge was at the end and then the hall branched to the left. I'd picked up my bucket and was going into the lounge when – down that left branch – I saw two feet: toes down, sticking out of a doorway.

I walked towards them. There was another surge of music. It was the chicken song. The feet went side to side. I kept walking. The music stopped and the feet went still. I had no idea what I was doing. I looked into the room. A man was on the floor wearing a business shirt, boxer shorts, and one sock. It was as if he'd been hit over the head while changing. There was an unmade bed covered in CDs and more CDs on the floor.

'Hey,' I said.

He didn't move or say anything.

I looked down the hallway. It was empty. The only sound was the far away flush of a toilet. I used my heel on his toes.

'Aah,' he said, and rocked side to side to get his foot free. He rolled onto his back. There were blotches on his forehead and nose from where they'd been pressed against the carpet. He was holding a remote control. 'Whoa,' he smiled. 'Welcome.'

His eyes made a slow revolution around the ceiling. He looked like the woman by the car.

'Where's your wand?' he said, making a gun out of his fingers. 'If you don't have a wand how can you grant me a wish?' The rest of him was still. He looked deflated, as if the part I couldn't see had sunk some way into the carpet.

'Don't point at me,' I said. There was a clock on the wall. I had to pick Tom up from the hospital. I looked back down the hallway. 'Move your feet,' I said.

'You have bad manners for a genie,' he said.

'Move your fucking feet.'

He bent his knees. 'What have you got in your bucket?'

I closed the door. He'd been lying on the leg of a pair of pants. The rest of them were under the bed. The belt looked expensive. I pulled at them with my toe and they came out. One of the pockets was bulging. 'What's that?' I said.

'Huh?' he said, licking his lips. 'Hey, what sort of genie are you?'

My heart felt so close to the surface I thought if I looked I'd see its shape. I bent over, wriggled the wallet out of his pants, and put it into the bucket. The music started again. It gave me a fright and I stood up. More CDs fell off the bed onto the floor. I opened the door. The man's feet shot forward like small dogs trying to escape. They started moving in time with the music. He was smiling and his eyes had focussed. 'What's wrong with you?' he shouted. 'Don't you like to party?'

I went out into the hallway. The music stopped. He was laughing. I started running. The front door was wide open. The grass was already under dew. The cold air was good. I got into my car and made a U-turn. There was a sound. I thought someone had thrown something at the car. I drove a little further and then stopped. I looked in the rear-vision mirror. It was getting dark; the hills were black smears. I rolled down the window and listened. 'Who's that?' I said.

A dog started barking. I got out of the car and threw

the wallet as hard as I could. It landed on the footpath and skidded onto the lawn where my footprints were like insect tracks. Where I'd turned the car there was a little glistening patch. The woman must have left the wine glass on the roof. A light went on in an upstairs room of the house. It was like a monster's eye.

★

Now Tom has a sister. This morning she and my husband were atop a slide watching a man emptying the park's rubbish bins. At the bottom of the slide she asked my husband what the man was doing. He told her about jobs and she told him she was going to be an electrician, but with wings.

He tells me this when they get home and I smile and sip the tea he's made me. Our daughter starts crying and when he goes to her I look out the window. Our house is high on a hill. Clustered around the harbour below are the city's grey buildings, and spreading out from them are the people's homes. Tonight, before sleep, I will sit with her on her bed. We will turn out the lights, make a crack in the curtains, and breathe long clouds over the glass. Then she will hold my finger like a pen and draw pictures in the sky.

Argentina

Todd and Rainey had gone to the camping ground's kitchen hoping to find some food, but there were only tea bags, cooking oil, and a little salt. The kitchen was a converted rail carriage and was well lit by two bare bulbs. Opposite the small table where they sat a bench ran the length of the carriage. There was a sink at one end of the bench and an oven at the other. Above the sink a window looked across a lawn to a cabin that was adjacent to the one Todd and Rainey had rented.

'Maybe we should drive back?' said Rainey. 'There's food at my flat.'

Todd sat even closer. He put one arm around her shoulder and the other around her waist. 'But it's getting dark,' he said, 'and I love our little cabin.'

They'd met at a come-as-your-middle-name party the Saturday before. Todd had been in the laundry winding toilet paper around his hands. Rainey had come in with a bag of chips. They'd got talking. Since then, excepting a few lectures, they'd spent every minute together. They talked a lot about their first year of university, about high school and about their childhoods. Whenever they found a thing in common, whether it be sharing a favourite flavour of ice block or agreeing on an issue related to climate change, they would kiss and cuddle and say things like, 'Isn't this amazing? Aren't we lucky?'

The day before, when they'd arrived at the cabin, Rainey had taken a red candle and a hardcover book out of her bag. She'd lit the candle and put the book beside the bed.

'Just what the room needed,' said Todd, kissing her.

It had been exciting having somewhere of their own and instead of drinking the wine and just eating the boiled eggs Rainey had brought, they'd eaten the eggs, drank the wine, and then gone to the pub where they spent the weekend's money on two fish meals and a lot of beer.

'It's the righteous thing to do,' Todd had said when they were agreeing to spend their last ten dollars. Earlier in the cabin Rainey had had an orgasm with him for the first time. They'd had sex before, but Todd didn't have much experience: sometimes he came very quickly, other times his hard-on went away at the wrong moment. He'd been worried about not being a good lover, but having performed, and full of food and beer, he felt like he and Rainey were on their own planet and that everything on that planet was happy and very beautiful.

The next morning they'd woken with hangovers. They laughed about what they'd done and about how crazy they were.

'What are we going to eat?' they giggled, holding each other close.

'Grass?' said Todd.

'Worms,' said Rainey. 'Worms and bird's nests.'

'We'll make a salad,' said Todd.

When they woke again it was early in the afternoon. There was the sound of sheep outside and then a shower of rain against the roof. Rainey had her back to Todd, but he could tell she was awake. He put his hand on her stomach and then further down. Her pelvis shifted away from him. He stopped. 'What are you thinking about?' he said.

She said she was feeling sick from the alcohol and that she was hungry. Then she moved his arm and reached for her book. Todd rolled away and pretended to go back to sleep. They'd prided themselves on never doing anything but talking, drinking, and messing about in bed. After a while he left the cabin and went across to the toilet block. When he came back she was looking at her cell-phone. He didn't want to feel suspicious. Love was meant to consume that sort of thing. He got into bed and stared at her imagining she was a glass of water and that he was a man lost in the desert. I thirst for you, I thirst for you, he chanted to himself. She stopped using her phone and stood up. She said they should go for a walk.

They went out of the camping ground, across the railway lines and into the town. There wasn't much to see. Outside the church a tall man was using a lawn mower.

'Is that him?' said Todd.

'Who?' said Rainey.

Todd had never been in love before, but Rainey had. In her last year of high school she'd been in love with a basketball player. Todd swaggered in a circle around her, dribbled, then aimed a shot at a street sign. Rainey watched but didn't say anything. He faked to one side and then went past her. 'Slam dunk for the big man,' he announced.

But she wasn't watching anymore; she was looking up and down the road. The day before, the sky had been high and blue. It had looked like it was stretched so tight that a sharp point would cause it to burst, exposing all the stars and the moons and the endless galaxies. When Todd said that to her she'd laughed and said, 'That's clever. I love the way you look at things.' Then she'd moved close to him and put her hand under his T-shirt.

As they walked back from the church the sky was grey and low and though he thought hard, Todd couldn't think of an interesting way to describe it.

A gravel driveway looped between the toilet block and the carriage. There was a car out there. It left the gravel and there was the gentler sound of it on the lawn. Todd got up from the table and went to the window. The car had stopped in front of the cabin. 'A car,' he said.

'I'm going to the toilet,' said Rainey.

'I'll miss you,' Todd said. After he'd convinced her to stay they'd had cups of black tea and looked at the pamphlets that filled the narrow plastic shelves beside the table. There was one about the Rail Trail: it had information about the length of the trail, where you could spend the night, and how to rent a bike. Another one promoted and featured the menu of the pub they'd been at the night before. After a while other than Todd mentioning the sounds Rainey's stomach was making – he'd joked that it was like a cat crying down there – they stopped talking altogether. Three nights before, having talked non-stop for eight hours, they'd joked about the impossibility of running out of things to say. 'Only if,' Todd had laughed, 'someone put a trowel through the talking part of our brains.'

A light went on in the cabin and a man crossed the room with what looked like a sleeping bag. Todd went out of the carriage and towards the back of the toilet block. World music was coming from the car. Rainey would like it – she'd been to New Plymouth once to see the different bands. It was one of three places in New Zealand she'd been to that Todd hadn't. Moving his feet Todd tried to find the rhythm in the music. If it had been yesterday he and Rainey might have done a little dance – she would have held her hair up and he could have rested his hands on her narrow hips. The man came out of the cabin. He waved at Todd and, walking around to the car's boot, said something Todd didn't understand. The man bent over the boot. He had a wide round bottom that didn't fit the rest of him. Todd smiled. A man with a woman's bottom – just the sort of thing Rainey would find funny. The toilet door closed. Todd went quickly to the back of the toilet block. He heard her footsteps on the gravel and then she walked past, shaking her hands as if to dry them. 'Aaarrrrrgghhhh!' he shouted.

She jumped as if a motorbike had back-fired and spun around. Todd had his arms up like the boogie man. Straight away he wished he'd stayed in the kitchen.

'Enough!' she said, wearing a look he'd never seen before. Then, when he walked towards her, she said, 'Can't you switch it off for a moment, Todd? I'm so hungry I could eat . . .' she looked around and motioned at the dark wet ground. 'Grass, I could eat grass.'

'And bird nests?' he said quietly.

'Pardon?' she said, tilting forward.

She reminded Todd of a teacher he'd been scared of. 'It doesn't matter,' he said.

Her face softened and she started to say something, but then shook her head, turned, and went in the direction of the cabin.

The car door closed. The man had a shopping bag in each hand. He was looking at Todd. Todd tried to smile nonchalantly, but felt his face sliding. He went back into the carriage and sat at the table, then stood and went to where, if he leaned close to the glass, he could see their cabin. The light was on, but he couldn't see her. At least her car was still there. His insides noodled about. He saw himself on the road the next day with his thumb out, holding the cloth bag he'd brought to carry his clothes. There'd be sheets of rain and then probably a typhoon.

There was a sound on the stairs. It's her, he thought. But it was the man from the cabin. One bag was full of potatoes, the other had milk, butter, and cooking utensils. The man smiled and said, 'Hi,' with a thick accent, then lifted the bags as if to put them on the bench and as if to ask if that was okay with Todd. Todd just nodded and went and sat where the pamphlets were scattered about on the table. The man filled a pot with water and set it on the element. Then he put the butter and milk on the bench. There were almost two litres of blue-top milk and the spout of the bottle was filled with creamy froth. Todd imagined one gulp after another. He'd take a large glass over to Rainey. For that cat in your belly, he'd say.

The man was laying the utensils on the bench: a whisk, a small and then a large knife, a peeler, a masher. Todd picked up one of the pamphlets and stared past it. It was the first time they'd been near but not together. The potatoes rumbled into the sink. Todd looked up. The man was watching his reflection in the window. Todd went back to his reading. The man came over holding the peeler. He raised his eyebrows at the pamphlet, pointed at Todd, and made an up and down motion as if riding a bicycle over bumpy terrain. 'No,' said Todd. 'Just here for the weekend.'

'?'

'The weekend. I'm a student. Me and my girlfriend . . .' Todd gestured to the place where he and Rainey had had the argument, 'We're students.'

'Students,' said the man through his thick accent.

'Students,' said Todd. 'From Dunedin.'

'Argentina,' said the man, putting his hand over his heart. There was a thumb-sized map of New Zealand on the Rail Trail pamphlet. The trail and its surrounds were highlighted in a light blue box. The man pointed to the box and from there swung the peeler over the Pacific until he hit South America, where, on the table top, he delicately traced the Chilean coast and then the long talon of Argentina.

'Argentina,' Todd repeated, trying out the pronunciation.

'Si,' whispered the man, 'Argentina.' After a moment he made a carrying motion from Todd to where he and Rainey had argued and back again. 'Aaah . . . disaster?' he said.

Todd shrugged. 'We've only just met, but . . . I love her.'

He'd told her the night before on their way back from the pub. He'd been lying on the railway tracks pretending he couldn't move, staring fearfully down the rails as if a locomotive were looming, and then, on one knee, clutching her thighs, he'd looked up and said it.

The man shaped his mouth down and shook his head as if he'd been in the same situation many times. Then shrugging expansively he went back to the sink where he started peeling the potatoes. He worked quickly. Peel went in all directions. The sound was of paper being ripped or of some animal munching wet vegetation. When he'd finished a potato he sent it tumbling and slithering in the direction of the oven. Soon they were a large flock − their carved faces glistening in the bright light. The water in the pot had started to boil and he halved then quartered the potatoes before dropping them carefully into the pot.

The steam softened the hard light. It became warmer. Todd was hungry, but no longer hungover. Fasting, he thought, I'm sharpening my brain and my body. He raised his arms above his head, lowered them slowly as if holding a huge bell and then flexed the muscles in his young legs. Before Rainey there was a tutor he'd been into. She wore eye make-up and long skirts. The Wednesday before the party she'd come up to him at the pub holding a jug of dark beer and smelling of weed. 'Todd,' she'd said, 'I bet *you* know how to spell assassin.' She'd left as he was answering, but he was sure there'd been something between them. The man bustled out of the carriage with the small knife and returned with a large sprig of parsley. 'Perejil,' he said in his language, and then again, holding up the herb and saying the word slowly.

'Perejil,' mimicked Todd. The man smiled. 'Argentina,' said Todd clenching his fist.

'Argentina,' cried the man as if they were at a protest. He put the parsley on the bench and took up the large knife. It had a blue handle and a broad blade and after cleaning it with a soldier's care he went to work. There was the cutting of the parsley and the machine-gun sound of the knife on the board. Todd got up and stood by the oven. He'd never seen anything like it. The man spun the board and went at a new angle. Soon it was all over. He put down the knife and, crouching so he was level with the bench, plucked again and again at the herb – and with that motion, like he was taking many small things from a magician's hat, he shaped the herb into a perfect green mound. Finished, he stood and made a smoking gesture and looked questioningly at Todd.

'No thanks,' said Todd.

The man patted Todd on the shoulder, squeezing the muscle in a comradely way, and then left the carriage.

Steam crawled across the ceiling. Outside the music started. Todd went to the window and wiped at the condensation. By the car there was a flame and then the lit end of a cigarette. He wiped more of the window and looked down to the cabin. She was there – standing in the window watching the man, and just as he'd imagined, she was moving in time with the music. One morning before sunrise he'd lain in bed while she danced. She had long strong legs and when she did anything with her arms her ribcage was visible as were the goose bumps over the underside of her arms and small breasts. The tutor and the basketballer flew out of him like crows caught in a bushfire. He went quickly towards the door of the carriage.

Before he got there it opened. The man came in. He had a folded square of cloth, which he handed to Todd. 'I have to go,' Todd said. 'I've got this all wrong.'

The man made the sound of someone trying to sooth an injured horse and cleared the pamphlets from the table. 'Si,' he said, pointing at the cloth. Todd handed it back. The man unfolded it and threw it across the table. A perfect fit – it was white with the red outline of a huge steak in the middle. 'Monseñor,' said the man, pulling a chair from the table, bowing slightly and making an encouraging sweep with his arm.

'But –' said Todd.

The man stood with his feet together and one hand on the back of the chair. There wasn't going to be an argument. Todd allowed himself to be seated. The man went quickly to the oven where he drained the potatoes and turned the element off. He cut a broad square from the butter dropped it in the potatoes and then grabbed a tea towel and, gesturing once more for Todd to stay exactly where he was, left the carriage. Todd got up from the chair and went to the window. The man was crossing the lawn. At the door of the cabin he took a moment to lay the tea towel across his left forearm, then he knocked. There was movement in the cabin and when she opened the door, her svelte shape.

She crossed first, then the man – following behind and just off to the side as if he was worried she might turn and run for it. Todd looked into the pot. The butter was falling through the potatoes. On the bench the utensils were laid out like surgical instruments. There was the parsley, the milk and three bowls. He went back to the table, knowing not only what the man was going to serve them, but how he, Todd, was going to position himself at the table, what he'd say when she walked in, and indeed, what he'd do and say for the rest of that night and all the days and nights to follow.

Racquet

When they'd bought the house the backyard had been a ramp of boggy lawn spotted with moribund bushes and trees. Leighton had transformed it by the close of summer. Now there were three tiers, steps in between, a vegetable garden, native shrubs, and a long bench wide enough for two.

He left the table and looked off the end of the deck. On the day he finished the bench they lay there entwined, pointing out faces the sky made in the leaves of the neighbour's gingko tree. He turned around. Sonya was still staring into her cup. He didn't know what to say. A tennis ball was on the chair next to her. 'Throw me the ball?' he said, quietly.

She looked at him. He used to skite that their brains were woven like a two-coloured frosty boy.

'Right in here,' he said, holding his left hand like it was a mitt.

She stood up. When they were courting they would go for walks along beaches and river banks. He would juggle two stones and a muesli bar. 'Poser,' she would laugh, and then she'd scoop water at him until he chased her, 'ooh aaring' around the muesli bar clamped piratically between his teeth. Afterwards he would show her how to throw: a straight left arm, a long stride, rotate the torso and whip your shoulder, elbow and forearm through.

The cup came at him and he ducked. There was the sound of it in the branches then a popping as it broke.

'Good one,' he said.

'Fuck you,' she said, and went into the kitchen.

While he'd worked on the garden she'd supervised the removal of an internal wall, the relocation of a stud, the building and furnishing of the deck. When the builders left she ripped up the carpet and sanded and treated the floorboards. After that there was wallpaper to strip and a scheme of colour to put down. There was month after month of it. At the end of every day they would lead tours of their respective realms:

'Should I plant spinach *and* silverbeet?'

'I need an extension for my roller.'

And at night he would trace his fingers over the dried paint on her arms and they would whisper so close that even the mice would miss the occasional word.

Now the kitchen flowed into the lounge, and she crossed the room with long strides and slammed the bedroom door so hard the dirty cutlery shifted in their dessert plates. He went to the seat and picked up the ball. He bounced it once. There was a light breeze. It went through his backyard with a sound like the strands of a foil skirt against a woman's skin.

The work was finished. There was a German fridge and a special shelf for the aquarium she'd promised herself. They'd talked for a long time about a skylight and now with a long kinked wand you could open a window they'd had cut into the roof iron – with patience a person could sit at the dining table and see rescue helicopters, chip packets, and once a bunch of balloons.

There was a knock on the front door. 'Miriam,' said

Leighton. The gingko was hers and now also the remnants of their cup. Crossing the lounge he lobbed the ball towards his squash gear. It was Tuesday, and on Tuesdays he played squash with Matty. He opened the door.

'Something exploded in my yard!'

Miriam was American. Leighton called her a Jewess though he wasn't entirely sure what that meant. She had dark hair and a nose like a gull's wing.

'A cup. Sonya and I were playing Donkey. She got one past me. I'll collect the fragments in the morning.'

'Donkey?'

He heard Sonya draw the curtains in their bedroom. It wasn't yet eight p.m. 'It's a catching game.'

'It's popular?' She was an art dealer or a designer. They were not sure which.

'It's just a game.'

'I don't want you in my yard in the morning. A man lurking in a woman's yard is likely to get shot.'

'A yardbird,' he said.

'I'm sorry?' She leaned like a farmer with one hand on the door frame and the other on her hip. Leighton could see beneath the sleeve of her T-shirt. Once, when he was working in the backyard, he'd seen her in her window. She was standing on one leg with her arms ravelled high over her head.

'A yardbird. It's an American term right?'

'I'm from New York.'

He'd told Matty about her yoga. She wants it, Matty had said. All that nude yoga, 1960s stuff is coming back big time. Matty was their accountant though he liked to be introduced as a moneyman.

'Shall I email you?' Leighton said.

'What?' She looked like he'd chundered into a pram she was pushing.

'The fragments. About a good time to retrieve them?'

'You know,' she said, 'I once rode a mule into the Grand Canyon.'

He noded, not knowing what to say.

She looked him up and down. 'A Def Leppard T-shirt and white shorts?' She stepped back and held out her hands in what Leighton thought of as a Jewish gesture. 'You dress for this donkey?'

Leighton smiled. He knew his wife would be listening. Once they would have laughed – sat on the end of the bed and giggled their way to hysteria. Then they would have started in. Now, for Pavlovian reasons, laughter and hard-ons often went together. But then he wondered if it was Miriam. He liked the hair in her armpits.

'I'm playing squash,' he said. 'I better go.' He started closing the door. 'Don't worry about that cup.'

'Worry?' she said. 'Why would you tell me not to worry?'

They always played the best of five sets. On this night, because Leighton won for the first time, there came a turning point.

It was a set all and Matty was serving for the third at eight points to six. He served across the court and down Leighton's backhand wall. Leighton stepped forward and played a drop shot back across the court. Matty, who was heavily built though agile – like a rat on Viagra, he'd say – surged forward, holding the face of his racquet out and flicking the ball over the tin with a desperate lunge. The ball sat up in the middle of the court and Leighton, who'd been poised just forward of the T, stepped in and hit a long arcing ball back to where Matty's serve had been directed. Matty stampeded across the court, hairy and muscular in his lucky lime-green shorts, and whipped an incredible shot back up the wall. Leighton, who'd relaxed thinking the point was his, thrust out his racquet and made a weak volley. With a

112

satisfied grunt Matty stepped forward and speared an even more precise backhand down the same wall.

Matty and Leighton were both similarly skilled and fit, but Matty always won. Sonya – a farmer's daughter and ex-sprinter – said it was because Matty was tougher. 'He's a mongrel and he'll suffer more. Have you ever tried killing a possum?'

For once, though, Leighton hurled himself into the back corner and swung without fear. His fingers jammed and left blood on the back wall. His feet went into the air and the racquet shifted in his hand. But enough of it caught the ball, looping it down the court like a poisoned fly. Prone on the floor he heard Matty's astonished yelp and watched him lurch to where the ball would kiss the front wall. Leighton scrabbled back to his feet. From the way Matty's racquet was angled he knew he was going to send the ball short to the forehand court and he swooped: like a cannon attack his feet pelted over the wooden floor and then crack! He thrashed that ball cross-court and up to the bloodied back-hand corner. Matty didn't move. He just gasped like a bayonet victim then looked in a surprised way at Leighton who, his brain shot high with adrenaline, tipped onto the heels of his feet, pumped his arms, and roared at the ceiling's bright lights.

'Jason Alexander,' said Leighton.

'Who?'

'Off Seinfeld. The guy off Seinfeld.'

'The one with the hair?' said Matty.

'No, with the glasses. The stumpy one.'

They were in the racquet club's bar, directly above the changing rooms they'd used after their match. Still wet from the shower, Matty had said, 'We're having a drink mate. You can't do that to a man and not have a drink.'

Leighton had nodded as he pulled on a sock. There was no reason to rush home and anyway, he felt good.

The barman – he'd once played in a Davis Cup tie against Ceylon – had been pleased to serve them. 'And look,' he'd said, walking around the bar, past the high empty tables, and to the windows where there were views of floodlit tennis courts. 'Geisha.' Three Asian women in tennis skirts were playing American doubles. The barman told a vagina joke – it involved making a nest of his hands – before going back to a stool in front of the bar where there was a cordless telephone and a phone book. But with each beer they ordered he became more agitated, finally exploding and pointing his watch at them like it was a ray gun, 'You know this isn't some sort of carnival.' Which was when Matty negotiated the six bottles of beer – 'I'll have to take the lids off and don't tell me the beer will go flat. It's the bloody law.' Then the barman pulled a screen down in front of the bar, sat the spare stools on the empty tables, and stomped down the stairs.

Now, while the tennis players stood around an umpire's chair, Leighton, who was normally deferential, chipped at Matty about his body-type. 'George Costanza,' he said. He got up and did a penguin-walk, waddling with his hands as flippers and like ears for his hips.

'Jesus, you're in a mood tonight,' said Matty, draining a beer and racking it with the other empties. 'Here, see you at the bottom.' He gave Leighton a full bottle and took one for himself. He raised the bottle and Leighton, now no longer laughing, clinked his against Matty's and brought it up to his mouth. The beer spluttered down his throat and reached into his nose. He looked at Matty who was cross-eyed but into the last quarter. Leighton tried to drink faster. It felt as far up as the back of his eyes then it was on his chin and making drips on the front of his T-shirt. Matty hammered his bottle on the table so the triangle of empties rattled.

Leighton winced and shook his face. 'God,' he said, 'arrgh.'

'One more?' said Matty, making a belch like a raven's cry and holding another bottle at Leighton.

'Eh?' said Leighton, smiling and putting his hands in his pockets.

'I gotta get home,' said Matty. 'C'mon mate, *you* won.'

So Leighton skulled one more. He went slower and didn't bother watching Matty. He took small gulps. It felt bad going down and when he finished he opened his eyes. Matty was no longer there.

'Next Tuesday,' said Matty from the doorway.

And then he was gone. Leighton coughed and there was a spewy taste in his mouth. He put the bottle on the table. The Asian women were coming across the court. In white frocks and singlet tops, with tight shiny ponytails switching side to side, they were laughing with their hands over their mouths.

'Right then,' said Leighton, picking up his bag and racquet and heading for the stairs.

He couldn't remember making a conscious decision to stop. One moment he was driving, and yes, looking, and then he was stopping and, using the panel on the driver's armrest, lowering the passenger window.

She didn't say anything, just looked into the car. There was something about her skin.

'Um,' said Leighton.

'I don't do um,' she said.

Leighton looked into the rear-vision mirror and then out the front of the car.

'Don't stress,' she said, 'they went by a while ago. Shall I get into your nice car?'

Leighton nodded. He was worried his voice would come out as a squeak.

'It's sixty dollars for a blowjob. Hundred and forty for the lot.'

Leighton cleared his throat. 'Where shall I go?'

'I want the money first,' she said.

He showed her his wallet and she got into the car and closed the door. He gave her three twenties and she put them into a black bag that had a safety pin instead of a zipper.

'Let's go to your place,' she said.

'Oh,' he said.

'I'm joking,' she said. 'Don't worry, I'm not like some of the other girls.'

Leighton didn't know what she meant. She was shorter than Sonya. He wanted to tell her to put her seatbelt on.

'Go down Grafton Road. There's a place beside the Caltex.'

He pulled the car away from the curb. Another woman was sitting on a low wall in front of a hedge. She was dark skinned and wearing a tight white skirt with a wide belt and cowboy boots. She was more of what he'd imagined.

'Do you play tennis?' said the girl. She had reached into the back seat and was holding up his racket.

'Squash,' he said. 'It's a squash racquet.'

She stood the racquet up on the back seat. In the rear-vision mirror, with its black cover, it could have been a passenger's head.

'Are you drunk?' she said.

Leighton stopped at some traffic lights. At a Mobil station a man was pumping petrol into a boat. 'A little,' he said. 'I won.'

'My hero.' The skin on her cheeks was shiny like it had been glazed. Underneath, around her mouth and on her cheek and jaw, the skin was flaky. 'Green,' she said, putting chap-stick on her lips.

He went through the intersection. Farther ahead he could see the red of the Caltex station.

'Can I turn on the radio?' she said.

He nodded and she turned the radio on and then expertly changed stations. It was a song he hadn't heard before. She sang some of the words and pointed across the road. 'There,' she said, 'down there.'

He indicated and stopped in the middle of the road. The indicating arrow on the dash flashed and clicked off and on. He hadn't done anything yet.

She looked at him. 'I'm not giving the money back. Do you want it or not?'

He accelerated. The underside of the car caught the pavement with a grated rock sound. Then they were going down a narrow alley with graffited fences on each side. The alley widened into a round gravelled lot. With the security lights from the surrounding buildings it could have been dawn. There was a bike frame in a puddle and a plastic rubbish bag against a wire fence. Leighton parked and turned off the ignition. The music went off. She opened her door and spat something out of her mouth. 'Well,' she said, turning back to him.

He thrust his hips up, undid his belt and fly, and slid his jeans and underwear down.

'I only do it with condoms,' she said, 'and that won't go on until you're hard.'

He looked at her.

She gestured in a way that reminded him of Miriam. 'You didn't pay for a hand-job.'

It was shrivelled back in the fur and he took it at first with his fingertips. He closed his eyes. Sonya was there and he opened his eyes. Usually he would spit onto his hand, but his mouth was dry and anyway it wouldn't seem right. There was the mosquito-whine of nearby neon and the sound of an air conditioning vent. He worked a little harder. The girl was getting something out of her bag and humming the tune from the song that had been playing. He tried closing his eyes again. It was better this time and he thought about the way they'd held their hands over their mouths when they laughed.

'Okay,' she said.

A car was parked in his usual spot. Leighton swore, sped up the road, and did a U-turn. There was a space opposite Miriam's house. He was desperate for a piss and since dropping the girl off had been holding the stem of his penis. Still holding on, he rushed diagonally across the road, through the gate, and down the side of his house. He stopped on the first tier, unbuckled his belt and started on the fly. But when the girl had finished he'd buttoned his fly incorrectly. It caused a delay. There was the wet warm feeling around his crotch, an erratic spray as he yanked his trousers down, and finally a long sigh as he took command.

He was wiping his hands on the lawn when the door to the deck opened. Sonya. He scuttled down the lawn, dropped onto the second tier, and concealed himself behind a pepper tree. There was the gentle lap of her bare feet on the wood and then the stretch of canvas as she sat down in the dark. Just before dropping the girl at the Mobil he'd asked about the condom wrapper. He was worried she'd left it in the car. He'd regretted the question straight away, but then been relieved when she dug into her purse. She'd brought her hand out of the bag knuckles up and then slowly rotated her hand extending her middle finger. 'Loser,' she'd said, getting out of the car.

There was the sound of his wife standing up and her chair going back. The same sound was repeated three more times and then the wood on wood shriek of the table being dragged across the deck. A light went on in Miriam's house and then the door to her deck opened.

'Hello?' she said. 'Who's out there?'

There was silence for a moment and then Sonya spoke. 'I'm over here,' she said.

'Sonya?' said Miriam.

'Yeah.'

He saw Sonya's shape by the bird-feeder. She had her hand on the back of her neck.

'I heard something,' said Miriam. 'I was going to call the police.'

'I was shifting the table.'

'Then I thought it might have been an opossum.'

There was quiet.

'Your husband's car is opposite my house,' said Miriam.

Worried they would see the moon glow of his pale face Leighton looked down. The wet patch in his crotch was cooling.

His wife hadn't answered.

'Your husband's car?' said Miriam again.

'We're okay here,' said Sonya. 'We don't need the police.'

He could see the top of Miriam's head and her hand on one of the pot plants that hung from the roof of her deck. 'Okay,' she said. 'I'll have to trust you.' Her door closed and the light went off. In the dark the pot plant's overflowing foliage was like the beards old men wear.

On his own deck his wife was standing on the table. Looking down or out he couldn't be sure. She looked tall and mighty as if she had a quiver of thunderbolts on her back. 'I know you're out there,' she said, as firm and clear as a newsreader. When she lay down all he could see were the outlines of her perfect feet.

Trees

I sit back into the inflatable chair and go gently across the pool. The kookaburras are still making a racket and Dad looks up as if it's me making the noise then goes back to his phone book. He's writing down the numbers of all the backpackers in Perth. My brother Carl has taken off. He'd been living at Grandad's place in Christchurch and from his note it sounds like he's depressed again.

Dad's cousin Coral collected us from the airport last night. She's the one who told us Carl was here. He rang her a few days ago, drunk apparently, and said he was staying at a backpackers in the city. When Coral asked for a contact number and if he wanted to come for a meal Carl told her not to tell Dad and then hung up.

I thought Coral was a little girl when I saw her at the airport. It wasn't until Dad leant down and gave her a kiss that I realised who she was. She's younger than I expected. I shook her hand. It was soft and she gave me a big smile.

'Lot of budget accommodation in Perth,' says Dad.

I just keep kicking from one side of the pool to the other. Me and Dad have been planting out a block of land and living in a holiday home in Palmerston, north of Dunedin. It's got red walls and a white roof. I call it the chilly bin. Dad thought that was funny to start with, but after a few months he didn't like me mocking anything we were doing. It's been a long winter and there's not much left to say to each other.

I roll out of the chair and into the water. It's quiet and cool and I hold my breath for as long as I can. When I come up the kookaburras are still going and the breeze is making a whispering sound in the eucalyptus tree at the end of the section. I am worried about Carl, he's my little brother after all, but it's good to be away from that forestry block.

Coral rang two nights ago while I was doing the dishes. I knew something had happened by the way Dad sat with the phone. Real tense like his whole body was listening. They didn't talk for long and then Dad called Grandad. He didn't even know Carl had left – apparently Carl often stayed the night at a mate's place. Dad made Grandad go to Carl's room and that's where he found the note. Grandad's a bit blind. He was finding it hard to read all the words and Dad was patient to start with, but then he got angry. Carl's had a few bad patches over the years and Dad would have been worried there was something in it about suicide. Still, that doesn't mean he should talk to his father like that. I went into my room and sat on my bed for a while. When I heard him hang up I went back into the lounge. Dad looked small – sitting with his knees together and his hands on his ankles. He usually fills a fair bit of space. It's the same when he drives: arm out the window – even in winter – and whenever we pass another truck he does the finger wave. I do the same thing when I drive.

I get out of the pool and lie on the concrete. It's almost too hot already. Dad's staring at something on the table.

'How's the pool,' he says.

'There are little spiders on the surface.'

He looks at me but doesn't say anything. A lizard zips down the wall of the house and up onto the barbecue. It stays there for a moment and I think about telling him, but then it disappears down the side and into some pot plants.

We left for Christchurch after the phone call. It was strange in the truck. We were wearing normal clothes and for some reason Dad had shaved so there was the smell of shaving cream. When we got to Grandad's he was in the kitchen, but the radio wasn't on and there were dirty dishes in the sink. The note was on the table. Dad read it standing up, still holding onto his bag. After he'd finished he let out a long breath and sat down.

'McDonald's rang for him today,' said Grandad.

'McDonald's?' said Dad.

'The restaurant people. He'd applied for a job as a cleaner.'

'A year at university and he wants a job at McDonald's?' Dad put his hands over his face. He still had the note and it was hard to tell if he was reading or crying. Grandad cleared his throat and asked me how the planting was going. I told him what we'd been doing and then Dad slid the note across the table. It said he was sorry for taking off and that he was going away. At the end it said he loved us. I guess that's what made Dad upset. Even though Carl's pissed around a lot, he is the youngest, and I don't know if this has anything to do it with it, but Dad's the youngest in his family too.

We sat around the kitchen for a while, then I got worried Grandad might cook us something and went to bed.

Dad's voice woke me. It sounded like he was watching a rugby game. I got out of bed and went halfway down the stairs. Carl and I used to pretend the staircase was a hydro-slide and at Christmas we'd wait there for Santa.

'I don't like living in that tiny bloody house, but I'm

trying to give him a start. He's a bloody dreamer.'

He'd never call Carl a dreamer. Even after all his cock-ups. I heard pots clatter and the tap going on. Grandad would be getting the porridge ready. He soaks his oats overnight. I heard him cough and he must have said something because Dad said, 'Freedom? It didn't do me much good did it?'

I've seen a photo of Dad when he was nineteen. We look pretty similar, though back then he had a beard. It went quiet in the kitchen then I heard a chair slide back and the radio was suddenly loud as the door opened. I went back up the stairs, but Dad must have heard me.

'Phil?' he said.

I just got into bed real quietly.

A phone's ringing next door and it's got the kookaburras working even harder. Dad puts his pen down and closes the phone book.

'What's the time?' he says.

'About eight.'

'No, what's the exact bloody time? I want to start calling these places at eight o'clock.'

'They're open all night,' I say, standing up and walking towards the house.

'Phil!' he says.

But I go inside. It's cool and dark with a low ceiling and blinds over the windows. At the sink the tap is a swivelling lever and after I've filled a glass I give it a good smack to turn it off.

I woke up this morning thinking I was still in Palmerston. Then I heard the birds. Out the window the sky was clear and pale. There was a park across the road. A jogger was running along a path that went into the trees. She was wearing one of those sports bras. I put on my shorts and running shoes and went quietly down the stairs and out the front door. It was warm already and the grass in front of Coral's house was like a mattress to walk on. I crossed the road and started to run. The eucalypt leaves crunched under my feet. I went past the woman and then swerved off the path and started side-stepping the trees. I almost fell over a kangaroo. It was huge and orangey and it looked around and then took off – travelling fast and low to the ground. In the distance there were others: waiting in a clearing with their heads over the grass or bounding through the trees. It was like another planet.

'Watch out for their shit!' said the woman, as she jogged past. She had blonde hair that flicked up when she ran.

'Been for a run?' Coral said, when I got back to the house. She was sitting by the pool in a blue robe.

When she drove us from the airport I'd sat in the back looking at all the cars on the motorway and then the signs on the shops. She and Dad were talking about Grandad's glaucoma and what had happened to Carl. Sometimes I watched her mouth in the rear-vision mirror.

'I saw some kangaroos,' I said.

She took a cigarette from a box on the table. 'There are a few of those around,' she said, smiling. 'How did you sleep?'

'It's warmer than Palmerston.'

'Do you like it?' she said, 'planting trees with your Dad?'

'It pays the bills,' I said.

Dad's started ringing the backpackers. Talking in the voice he uses when he's making a doctor's appointment. The first five or six turn up nothing and I get back into the pool and sit in the chair. Then Dad straightens and holds the pen over the paper. 'He left New Zealand without telling anybody. We just want to know if he's all right.' He must get put on hold because he looks at me with his hand over the bottom of the phone and says, 'Phil,' like he's about to tell me to do something, but then he raises his finger like he wants *me* to be quiet and starts talking again. There is a lot of noise from the birds and insects. It's different from the hill. Sometimes a lark might come flitting over, but usually it's so quiet you can hear the motorway which is miles back towards the coast.

'Found him,' Dad says, standing up. 'They're going to ask him to ring me.' He squats by the pool running his hand back and forth through the water. Dad's started carrying weight in the same places as Grandad. We've all got the same crooked nose.

'Eh?' he says.

But I didn't say anything.

'I'm going to have a shower and get myself ready. Have you had some breakfast?' he says.

I roll out of the chair and dive back under the water. I kick to the end, turn around, and do another length. When I come up for air he's gone.

Most mornings there's more farting than talking in the truck. We can go for whole days without saying much to each other. On the hill we get our gear together and go our separate ways. At morning tea Dad sometimes goes on about a hare he's seen, but mostly we sit, eat, drink tea and get back into it. Lunchtimes I pretend I'm having a snooze and in the afternoons we talk about what we need from the nursery or what's for dinner. Then we drive home, eat, watch television, go to bed, get up and do it again.

I lie on the concrete beside the pool. My arms smell of the chlorine and sometimes what I think are leaves turn out to be more lizards, but I only know for sure when they dart away. I start getting hot. When I stand up my shape's there. It starts disappearing from the outside in and the last bit left is the rectangle of my shorts.

'Phil! Jesus! Get yourself ready.' Dad's standing by the

barbecue, rubbing sunscreen into his ears. 'He could call at anytime.'

I go inside and put on some clothes. Dad's in the kitchen when I come down the stairs. There's an empty glass beside him and when he sees me he holds it up. I shake my head and go out to the table by the pool. Dad comes after me holding the phone and carrying the glass of water. I can't remember the last time I saw him wearing a shirt. 'Don't get dehydrated,' he says, putting the glass beside me.

I ignore him and the water and after a while he goes back inside. I can hear a television next door. I was eight the last time we were here. I can't remember much. There was a rollercoaster that Carl wasn't allowed on because he was too short and a cereal ad with a talking toucan. One day after we'd been to a cemetery and it was pouring with rain we saw thousands of little black frogs hopping along a gutter.

Dad comes out and right then the phone starts ringing. He points at it like I've never seen one before and when he answers he doesn't say hello or anything. 'Carl? Carl?' he says. 'It's Dad.' He's got his hand out in front of his body like he's expecting to catch a pineapple. He looks scared and Carl's obviously not saying anything cause Dad says his name louder this time and then looks at the phone. He holds it back to his ear and then stands up like he's grabbed an electric fence. He looks over at me and starts to talk, but then Carl must have said something to shut him up. 'He wants to talk to you.' He gives me the phone which is white with a pink knob at the end of the aerial.

'Hey,' I say.

There's no response. 'It's me,' I say.

'Yeah,' says Carl.

'Me and Dad are here.'

I hear him sniff.

'Ask if we can see him.' Dad's standing behind me. I sit back and feel his fingers against my shoulder.

'Can we see you?' I say.

There's more silence. I can hear Carl breathing then there's a sound like he's put his hand over the phone.

'Do you like it here?' I say.

'It's hot,' he says.

I laugh. 'No shit.'

'What's he saying?' Dad says.

'We're at Coral's place. She's got a pool.'

'Is he pissed off?' he says.

I look over my shoulder. Dad reaches for the phone, but I keep hold of it. 'He's just worried.'

'I'll meet you at two, at the Swan. It's a pub in the city,' he says. 'It's beside a sports store.'

'Okay.'

'See you Phil,' he says.

I hand the phone back to Dad and stand up.

'What did he say?'

'Two o'clock at a pub called the Swan.'

Dad takes my wrist and looks at my watch. 'How did he sound?' he says.

'Like Carl,' I say.

Dad shakes his head. 'Jesus,' he says

Dad has a bum-bag for his documents and money. When we get on the bus he spends ages digging around for the change. It turns out he's only got twenties and the bus driver says in a thick accent, 'You gotta be joking.'

Dad goes red and starts turning out his pockets. I've got some coins and after a while I step past and say, 'Two to the city.' I can tell Dad's really angry so I sit in a single seat and Dad stands there glowering until more people get on and he has to move. I look out the windows: there are men wearing cowboy hats, and cars with the steering wheel on the left-hand side, there are women in suits with sunglasses and high heels, and barefoot Aborigines in football jerseys. Any one of them beamed over to Palmerston would draw a real crowd.

We get to the pub just before one thirty. Dad was worried we wouldn't be able to find it or that we'd get lost so we left Coral's with plenty of time to spare. There are tables on the footpath. Dad sits down and I get the beer.

'Schooners mate,' I say, putting the beer on the table.

Dad takes a gulp.

'Do you remember when we saw the frogs?' I say.

'Frogs?'

'In the gutter, there were thousands of them. We'd been at a cemetery.'

He looks at me kind of strange but nods and he even manages a little laugh when I tell him about Carl not being allowed on the roller coaster. 'I had to buy him that platypus,' he says, looking up and down the street.

It's two o'clock and Dad's already sent me into the pub to check if Carl's magically popped out of a pokie machine. At two-fifteen Dad tells me to go back inside and make sure that the pub is known as the Swan and not by some other nickname. I point at a sandwich board on the footpath and at the huge writing on the pub itself. When Dad says that there might be another Swan in town, I point to the sports store next door.

'So what?' says Dad.

I tell him what Carl said about the pub being next to a sports store and of course he gets pissed off again. We sit for another half hour without talking. There are lots of people coming and going on the footpath, but none of them is Carl. After a little longer Dad goes to a pay-phone and rings the backpackers. Carl's checked out. They have no idea where he is.

I'm in the pool. Dad's on the phone updating Grandad. He's sitting forward and looking at the ground. The plate-sized bald spot on the top of his head is red and burnt looking.

We ended up staying at the pub until four o'clock – in case I'd heard Carl wrong – and the sun was right over the top of us. Dad would usually have done something about it, but he just sat there.

When he's finished on the phone I say, 'Reckon we might have a barbecue later?'

'Jesus Phil,' he says. 'This isn't Club Med.' Then he goes inside.

I wasn't being smart. Dad likes barbecuing. I thought it might take his mind off things. I float around in the pool for a bit and then I hear the garage open and close. Coral appears in the kitchen. She's singing and going through the mail. When she comes out to the pool she gives me a wave. 'A beer?' she says.

'Yes please,' I say.

She bows like she's on stage then goes back inside. I get off the chair and sit on the side of the pool. Coming back from the pub Dad told me that when we were last here we hadn't visited a cemetery. 'You two were too young for that sort of thing,' he said. I asked about the frogs and he said in a quiet way that he did remember the frogs, but that that was after we'd been at a mini-putt in the city.

Coral's wearing a yellow bikini. There are white spots on it and lines of creamy white skin around the edges. It's strange to think that when I first saw her I thought she was a little girl. She sits down beside me and hands me a can and a thing made with wetsuit material. I look at it. She holds her one up to her ear. 'Hello? Hello?' she says. Then she slides

129

it over her can. 'Bloody Kiwis,' she says, smiling at me. 'So? How did it go today?'

I tell her about calling the backpackers and waiting at the pub.

'What's plan B?' she says.

I shrug. 'Dad's inside.'

The can's big in her hand and her elbow brushes my forearm when she takes a drink. 'Poor guy,' she says. I don't know if she's talking about Dad or Carl so I don't say anything. After a while she points at my empty can and says, 'Another one?'

I get two more and when I come back out she asks me to get an ashtray and to bring her cigarettes which are on her dresser.

Her room is quiet and the wooden floor is cool under my bare feet. There's a mirror above the dresser and everything is neatly arranged. Photos, a box of jewellery, and then a little stack: a book, her cigarettes, a lighter. The room smells good as if someone's been stirring flowers and the sheets on her bed are smooth and black. I hear footsteps on the stairs and grab the cigarettes and go out of her room. Dad's in the hallway. He frowns and I hold up the cigarettes. 'Coral wanted these,' I say.

'Don't you bloody drink too much,' he says, staying in the middle of the hallway. He's got his arms out to the side and his face is red from the sun. For a moment he seems huge, and I have to get side on to get past him, but then, when we're face to face, his expression changes. 'He'll be all right, won't he?' he says, and it's like everything drains out of him. Before I can think of anything to say he goes into the room he's been sleeping in and closes the door quietly, and then, as if he's afraid of anything fast or loud, he slowly returns the door handle to horizontal.

I give Coral the cigarettes and sit down. She lights one

and when she inhales something moves in her neck. After a while she knocks me with her little body and says, 'Hey, cheer up,' and then, 'What are you making me for tea?'

I take a gulp of beer and then without smiling say, 'That's the woman's job.'

'Oh, listen to this.' She reaches into the pool and flicks water into my face.

I wipe my face and watch the surface of the pool go calm.

'How about a barbie?' she says.

Dad comes outside. His hair is sticking out like he's been lying down and he's holding up a can and pointing at it like he's on a beer advertisement. 'All right if I have one?' he says.

It's dark now and Coral and I are climbing the eucalyptus tree. She said we would be able to see the city. I had to give her a boost into the first branch, but after that she kept ahead of me. The bark is white and shiny and I can hear frogs going.

After Dad came out to the pool we all drank a beer together and then he and Coral went off to the shops. I wondered what Carl was doing and when they came back, and after we'd had some more beer, I said that to Dad. He was standing beside me and he shifted a chop on the hotplate then he drank from his beer and said to Coral, 'Never have children.'

Later on Carol raised her can and said, 'To finding him!' and I took a long skull and ended up with the hiccoughs. Coral told me to stand on my head and Dad told me to drink a bottle of water upside down. Just before he went to bed he put his hand on my neck and said, 'Thanks for your help today.'

Coral stops climbing and points. 'See,' she says, smiling down at me.

The buildings are tall and bunched and under a dome of light. I've got my arm around the trunk and with my other hand I'm holding the branch above. Coral's feet are on each side of my hand and when she shifts I feel the warm outside of her foot. I can still hear the frogs and further away a siren.

Carl and I grew up on a sloping three-acre section. There were pines on one side and a line of poplars down the other. One day Dad said he'd give us fifty cents if we could climb the length of the poplar line without touching the ground. We went to the top of the first tree and then clambered from one tree to the other. Halfway down the line there was a decent sized gap between two trees and we sat in the uphill tree for ages trying to work out a way across. There was a fence beside the poplars and we talked about using that as a bridge and then for a while Carl was poised to spring from one tree to the other. Dad came over and leaned against the fence. He didn't say anything, just looked at the downhill tree and back to us. He was smiling and shaking his head like we would never make it. Carl got angry and broke off a branch and threw it at Dad as if it was a spear. Dad dived for cover in the long grass and we pelted him for a while until eventually he raised his hands in surrender, climbed through the fence, and stood between the two trees with his legs and arms set wide.

People and animals

Benny drove into the Tunnel Beach carpark. His girlfriend, Carol, was in the passenger seat. It was a Tuesday afternoon, a work day, and other than an old van the carpark was empty. That morning Benny had asked his boss for the afternoon off and at two p.m. he'd driven to Carol's house. He'd planned to go in both barrels blazing, but on seeing her – kneeling, using long scissors on a swatch of fabric – with the sun making it appear as if her little torso was piped with gold, Benny instead explained how he'd found his boss, 'Shoes off, no tie, radio on', and then, with his usual increase in volume, 'you'd think he was at the bloody beach.'

'But what are you doing here?' Carol said, standing up.

It was Benny's first go at breaking it off with a woman and having fumbled his 'shock and awe' plan, and with the cosy room smelling good from some happening in the kitchen, he decided it was the wrong atmosphere for the forthright conversation he'd planned. 'Well,' he lied, 'when I saw Julius bloody Caesar there I told him I'd thrown up and that I was taking the rest of the day off.'

Carol stopped squeezing his elbow in the way he liked. 'And you came straight here?'

'You don't get many days like this in July,' he said, settling on a new approach. 'We're going for a drive.'

They'd been seeing each other since June. One of their first dates had been at Tunnel Beach. 'I love the drama of the place,' she'd said.

'Drama? That's a women's thing: *Shortland Street, Days of Our Lives*.' He hadn't thought he was joking, but she'd laughed and then made him sit – on the scruffy turf near the cliffs – in such a way as to allow her soft body to fit between his legs.

'Mr Bureaucrat,' she'd said, 'you intrigue me.'

Benny hadn't known too much about that – what he remembered most was the warmth off her and the way she raised the leg of his trousers and traced the surface of his knee with the tip of her little finger.

So, having come upon the turn-off to the carpark, Benny had turned, reasoning as he did that ending it at a beach was no better or worse than ending it anywhere else.

'Look,' said Carol, after they'd got out of the car and walked past the van. Its rear door was open – the insides exposed: a T-shirt, the side and corner of a bare mattress, two tins of food on a pillow. There was no order, as if there'd been tear gas, or as if sleepwalkers had slid back the door and wandered off. 'Where are they?' said Carol, shading her eyes. The T-shirt slipped onto the gravel, then, in the wind, shifted like foam towards a puddle. 'Uh oh,' she said, starting slowly towards the van. It was one of the things that frustrated Benny. At work, and in his daily life, he liked to hustle. He'd jog from his work station to a colleague's desk. Jog from the lifts to the teleconference room. It wasn't that he was ever late – it was more to do with state of mind, and what he thought, as he watched her retrieve the T-shirt, fold it carefully and place it on the mattress, was that his next girlfriend would need more of that Red Bull kind of attitude.

'Watch it,' he said, as she slid the vehicle's door home, 'those freedom campers use these places like public toilets.'

There is a tunnel at Tunnel Beach – a nineteenth-century gentleman with daughters who loved to bathe employed tunnelers to make a passage down to the sandy beach – but the area is known as much for the large, paw-shaped promontory that slopes high to low in the way of a full sail. From its highest edge you are sixty metres above the little beach that gives the place its name, while the view north, beyond the beach, and south, is of a coastline where paddocks give way to cliffs, tooling away at the base of which is the Pacific Ocean.

'I can't see the van-people,' said Benny. He and Carol were near the middle of the paw, looking back to the track down from the carpark.

'Maybe they're on the beach,' said Carol.

Benny just nodded. The track had been muddy. It was fenced on each side – black cows sat about on the steep paddocks in the way of those anticipating the resumption of a tedious performance – and Carol had gone down clutching the top wire as if her life depended on it. Ahead of her, waiting occasionally to call out instructions, Benny had had plenty of time to think. He'd made a mistake. If he did it here there'd not only be the walk back (he hadn't noticed its length the last time), but the drive. What if she started crying in the car?

'The seagulls,' said Carol, 'they must love it here.' She pointed at two gulls on the cliff's edge.

If her rate of motion got under Benny's skin this was the sort of comment that ended up in just the same place.

Seagulls are seagulls – they don't care where they are. They fly around looking for food to eat. That's it. She had this way of turning his comments back on him though. She wouldn't speak for a while and then she'd describe something she'd heard on the government radio, like how fish communicate using clicks. And then, with anything to do with people or animals, she always got it back to sex.

'Maybe we should go,' said Benny.

'Back?'

'It's cold,' he said, pocketing his hands in his suit jacket. He stamped his feet. One gull went up like a kite. The other tilted its head, flung out its wings and cried.

'Are you wearing your catsuit?' she said, smiling over her shoulder as she went towards the highest part of the promontory.

Carol ran her clothing alteration and repair business from the room at the front of her house. An industrial-sized sewing machine sat on a table, beneath which were a set of squat drawers – amongst many unidentifiable things, there were buttons, zips, and spools of red cotton like shotgun shells. Once, while Carol was getting herself ready, Benny tried to manhandle the machine. It's like an anvil, he'd thought, bending his knees and giving it go. Something shifted in its guts. It goaded him with a whirring sound. He put everything into it, but instead of going off the table it started to topple. He only just managed to save it.

Another time when he went to pick her up she was sitting in front of the machine. She was sorry to keep him waiting, but there was a job she had to get finished. She'd brought him a can of beer and he'd sat in a lounge chair behind her. This time he'd been relaxed. It was warm and the machine had hummed. When he woke up she was measuring his inside thigh.

. . .

Around Carol the sky was a cold, cloudless, far-off blue. 'It always reminds me of *Jurassic Park*,' she said, making wings of her arms.

Benny went up the slope, and he had to admit it, she was right. Where the waves broke there were rainbows and thunder and their broken water mumbled up the sand of the small beach that was punctured by dollops of rock. The beach itself was shaped like a halved, family-size pie – at the far end were a string of little islands (with spire-like rock formations) – and backed by sixty-metre cliffs, where, immediately below the paddock's edge, pigeons roosted, putting their heads through their feathers and staring coldly across the abyss.

'They don't look the sort for a van,' said Benny. *They* were an older couple. Sitting, hands on knees, on a small rock at the base of the cliff on which the birds perched.

'Looks like they are waiting for someone to take their picture,' said Carol, making a follow-me gesture and heading in the direction of the tunnel.

Benny thought of contradicting her. Saying no, he didn't bloody well want to. It might be the way into an argument he could punctuate by throwing his head back and saying, 'Oh, for Christ's sakes, I can't take this anymore!' She'd storm up the track while he brooded down below. He'd let her get out on the road, beyond the carpark, and then drive up to her with the window down. She'd swear and throw gravel. It would be the last straw.

He followed down the slope, back to where the track from the carpark ended, and to where the tunnel made a shaft through the rock. 'No,' he said, but not nearly loud enough.

The tunnel's ceiling was close and the air smelt cool and of kelp. Benny started down. Ahead of him the sunlight on the sand at the end of the tunnel made a halo around

Carol's head. She loved to play where the waves spilled up the beach, to hop and skip just out of their reach. One time she ran up and threw her arms around him, settling her face in his neck, and then, and this made him feel really good, she put the tip of her little nose into his ear and sniffed. Benny dragged his hands down the sides of the rock walls. He would've liked to shout, or laugh – to work on an echo. 'Pop, pop, pop,' he went as he took the last few stairs.

'Boo!' said Carol, reappearing, and then, without waiting, 'What are we doing here, Benny?'

'Eh?'

'What do you want to say?'

His brain flopped as uselessly as a fish on an escalator. 'Ah –' he said, blushing.

He'd had unimpressed looks from women before, but the one he now got from Carol really hit him in the chest, and all he could do was watch as she turned and hopped onto and then off the tail end of a huge rock – it was in the shape of a sleeping lizard – and crossed the sand towards the old couple. He started to follow but then went down the alley the rock made with the cliffs of the promontory. A wave came up the beach and he stopped. I should have stayed at work, he thought, and in thinking that, he had another, happier thought. He *was* wearing the catsuit. To be fair though he preferred to call it underwear; it didn't have a tail after all. Anyway, when she'd ambushed him at the end of the tunnel that's what he should have said.

The wave retreated and he scampered around the head of the rock. Breaking up could wait. With his mind made up he expected her to be right there but she wasn't, and another rock, this one in the shape of an upright clam, obstructed his view up the beach. A wave broke and in good spirits – suddenly he was a US Marine – he dashed up the beach and peered around the edge of the rock. Carol was there, standing behind the old couple. Benny couldn't hear what they were saying though it was clear they were talking happily – the older woman grinning, while the man gestured at Carol who started to laugh. Not in a subdued way, but as if her laughter were the power behind a machine that made flowers grow. Benny had never seen her like that before and he grinned. He couldn't help himself. And as he did the last piece of the previous month's puzzle slotted into place. He liked her. He really liked her!

He straightened his tie and, wishing he had a comb, put his fingers through his hair. He started to go to her, but then, having a better idea, he stopped and went back behind the rock where he took off his jacket.

The parcel had turned up in the mail a few days after he'd fallen asleep in her sewing room. Great, he'd thought, when he unwrapped it, underwear. Now she wants to be my mother. The next frosty morning though he'd tried it on. It was black and webby and at first he was confused by the lack of a mid-section. Thin strands connected the upper and lower sections, but the rear and the groin were totally uncovered. They were windows. 'No way,' he'd blustered at the mirror when he finally figured it out, then, in a whisper, surrendering to the pleasant squeeze of it and swinging into a slow twirl, 'No bloody way.'

Unbuttoning his shirt, he was still holding his jacket and tie. There was no obvious place to put them. My shoes, he thought, feeling pleased that despite his excitement his problem-solving skills were still sharp. He unlaced his shoes, stashed his socks, then folded his jacket and placed it with his tie on top of the shoes. He took off his shirt and added that to the stack. The sea air was a curious, invigorating tongue. It found the bare flesh above his belt line. He dug his toes into the cold hard sand. Mother earth, he thought.

He leaned into the rock and peered around the side. No

longer laughing, Carol was looking beyond him and out to the ocean. He went back behind the rock and straightened the stack of clothes. A gull cried. Another wave broke. He wiggled his toes. It was irresistible. Undoing his belt he pulled down his trousers and folded them onto the stack. He stood. His heart was up near the back of his mouth. He'd signal her to come over and thank her for the suit. She wouldn't believe her eyes. She'd be tickled. She'd definitely do that thing with her nose. He looked again and waved. The tip of his penis touched the rock face. They didn't see him. 'Carol!' He waved more furiously.

They looked. He ducked instinctively and then looked again.

Livestock fall from paddocks around New Zealand's coastline all the time. Most go over at night, but some, in this case the cow Benny saw as he signalled again to his girlfriend, fall during the day. There was the black speeding weight of it, a sound like someone blowing in an unskilled way into a cornet and, before the assertive bone emptying crack of its landing, a twisting that for a moment convinced Benny it was not an animal – not blood and guts at all – but some theatre prop inhabited by two pranksters.

Johnsonville

The three men went into the pub. They'd been on a driving range in Petone. Steve had watched Al and Glen practice their drives. It was late in the day and a lot of other men were practising. There were balls everywhere as if there'd been a storm of yellow hail. A man in an armoured buggy was collecting the balls. The buggy's nose was shaped like an old style lawn-mower, but instead of behaving like a mower – working round and round or side to side – it was tearing all over the place: past the spindly pines, out to the fringe of the range, through the boggy area towards the golfers. Steve was concerned about the armour. What if there was a chink and a ball got through?

At the pub they sat near a wide-screen television. There was a game on. Al, who was the shortest of the three and stocky, had drunk over a hundred pints of Guinness at the pub. Around the time he finished his hundredth pint, management changed the way they ran the pint-club. Now you needed to drink two hundred pints.

'That's why Al's name isn't on the wall with the other men,' said Glen. He'd been polishing his glasses. First he'd done the lenses, then each arm, and now he blew into the hinges that joined them to the frame. Al didn't say anything. He was watching the rugby. Glen held up the glasses and tipped them so they caught the light.

Steve felt he should say something. At the driving range he'd said, 'Good shot,' and, 'You got hold of that one!' But since then he hadn't said a thing. It was the first time he'd met Al. After the pub he and Glen were going to watch the test match at his flat. 'Do you ever come to this place on a Friday or Saturday night?' he said, looking at Al.

Al was coughing and blowing his nose. He was looking over the napkin at Glen. After they'd picked Al up and on the way to the range Al had sneezed over and over again. Glen had asked if it was swine flu. 'Shit no,' said Al, 'that lays you up for a couple of weeks.' Then he'd tilted his head back and sneezed again.

Al finished wiping his nose with the napkin and rolled it into a wet looking ball. 'I like Guinness,' he said, holding up his beer and pointing it at Glen. 'I like the taste of it. Why the hell would I care if I'm not on the wall?' Al had a loud voice.

A woman at the bar turned around. She was wearing an All Black jersey.

Glen smiled into the bottom of his empty glass and then stood up. 'Another one?' He put the tip of his finger on the rim of Steve's glass.

Steve and Glen had been drinking in the city the night before. Steve had a bad hangover. He knew he shouldn't have more beer, but the first one had made him less anxious. He nodded and shifted his empty glass. He'd left the nightclub without telling Glen and when he got home he'd sat in bed and watched a romantic comedy. What he would have liked from Al was a story about a man who'd come into the pub one night and met a woman who looked and smelt like she'd been on a shampoo ad.

'Why would two teams wear strips that are so fucking similar?' barked Al, staring at the television.

It was dark when they walked to Glen's car. On the main road there were lots of neon signs on different shops and restaurants. The unlit spaces, where there was an alleyway or a bush, looked black and deep like someone had been punching holes in the place.

Glen and Steve had decided on a takeaway dinner from the Roast Canteen, but Glen was having difficulty finding a park.

'For Christ's sake,' said Al from the back seat, 'park in KFC.'

Glen went around a roundabout and pulled into the carpark. Then he started in on a story about how when he'd stayed at Al's place, when he first arrived in Wellington, Al always bought a burger that contained two chicken fillets, bacon, and extra mayonnaise. When Glen mentioned the quantity of mayonnaise a second time, Al shouted, 'Is this Mastermind or something? Who remembers this sort of shit?' Then he blew his nose.

'Hey!' shouted Glen, looking into the back of the car. 'What did you blow your nose on?' As they'd left the pub Al had asked Glen if there were any tissues in the car. Glen had said there weren't.

Al sniffed. 'Go and get your tea,' he said.

Glen got out of the car and slammed the door. He started towards the shop. Steve followed. Across from KFC there was a petrol station and above that a sickle of moon. Steve stared at the part under shadow. It was mysterious. It was the type of thing you could share with a girlfriend.

'Oi!' shouted Glen, holding the door to the Roast Canteen open. 'C'mon!'

Glen got pork and Steve got lamb. They waited in front

of two drinks fridges for their orders to be filled. An Asian woman called out an order and a huge man who'd been sitting at the front of the shop got up. He had a tattoo on his neck and his shorts were like two Kleen-Saks stitched together. He walked out of the shop with a plastic bag filled with polystyrene containers.

'He's the sort of man the All Blacks need tonight,' said Glen, gesturing at the door. 'Someone with a bit of mongrel.'

Steve nodded. The fridges were buzzing and the tube lighting on the ceiling was bright.

At a table a man and woman were waiting. The man was leaning back in his seat and spinning an empty can. Each time it went around a little more liquid dribbled onto the table. The woman was going through the pages of a magazine like she was angry at something.

'See?' said Glen, 'that's what a relationship does to you.'

Steve had known Glen since university. The previous night, once they were pissed, Steve told Glen about the trouble he was having with his ex. Glen had listened for a while then when Steve went quiet he'd said, 'You know what you need? Sambuca!'

Steve shifted from one foot to the other and patted at the corner of his mouth like there was lint there. Earlier in the week, on the bus home from work, something had happened to his breathing. It had started as a sensation around his mouth like something electrical was being held there. He'd looked around, wondering if anyone else had noticed. It was raining and the bus was attached to the wires, but none of the other passengers seemed to have noticed. His chest was shifting slightly and his stomach was going in and out. He put one of his hands over his heart and the other over his belly like he was blocking an attack. His breathing got shorter and shorter. The tingling spread back to his ears. He wasn't sure if he was supposed to be bringing air in or taking air out. He pressed the button to stop the bus and went through the other passengers like they were bamboo. *Excuse me,* someone said. Outside he sat on a bench and counted the roofs of the houses. He watched a seagull land and take off. Whatever it was had passed.

'They deep fry the potatoes, but the rest is fairly healthy,' said Glen, nodding at the food.

A man was at one end of the counter carving the different joints of meat. Next to him a woman was filling steel trays with potatoes and kumara. The peas and carrots were kept warm in trays of hot water and a woman, who also took orders, stirred the special gravy. The man started with your choice of meat and by the time the polystyrene container reached the gravy-lady it was full.

Steve had the bag of food in his lap. He was looking in the rear-vision mirror as Glen reversed out of the carpark. Al was in the back corner with his pale face near the window. Steve was worried something would happen to his breathing while he was at Al's flat. It was Glen's car and he'd have to wait until Glen was ready before he could leave. If it gets bad, he thought, I'll go into Al's toilet and pretend to throw up. Then I'll tell Glen and ask if he can get me home. But Glen would want to watch the All Blacks. He'd talked nonstop about the forward pack the night before. Maybe he'd refuse to help.

When they stopped at a red light Al said he wanted beer.

'Haven't you got a cold?' said Glen.

'So?' said Al. 'Are you my mother now?'

'Well I can't drink,' said Glen. 'I have to drive. Are you going to drink?' Glen looked at Steve. With his long face and the way his head was turned he looked like a wolf. Before Steve could answer, Glen wound both the back windows down using the control panel on the driver's arm-rest.

'Fuck's sake,' bellowed Al.

The liquor store was a drive-thru. There were long orange poles holding a high roof. Lots of cars were parked and people kept going in and out. Steve was waiting in the car. He could see Al and Glen standing in front of a pyramid of beer boxes. Two women came out of the store. The first was wearing a white cardigan and had shimmering earrings. The box of alcohol she was carrying clinked. The woman beside her was jagged looking with prominent bones in her face. The first woman, heavier and set low like a tractor tyre sunk into the ground, was looking straight at Steve. She came closer. She was swaying. There was a glistening ring through her nose. He looked at the bag in his lap and then glanced back. She blinked slowly and put the box on the ground. He imagined them dragging him out of the car and, like in the cartoons, walloping him on top of the head so that his feet disappeared into the concrete. But nothing happened. They'd put their alcohol down to light cigarettes.

Glen and Al appeared. They were each carrying a box of beer. Al was laughing and he'd tilted his box and was ripping at its back end. They got into the car. 'Al said that if we want to get pissed we can sleep at his place.'

'Oh, I don't know . . .' said Steve.

'Remember mate,' interrupted Glen, 'you owe me after taking off last night.'

They were at the exit to the liquor store. They needed to cross the busy main road to get to the street Al lived on. Steve bunched and un-bunched his hands. It was one car after another. Glen edged forward. Steve could hear the beer in the neck of the bottle Al was drinking. A car turned off the main road and went around them. There were three men inside. The man in the passenger seat stared at Steve.

'Fuck's sake,' said Glen, edging the car further onto the road.

But the cars were endless: paced one after the other like each one was attached to the spokes of a wheel buried in the earth's core. Meanwhile, in Al's dark lounge, dominating the room with its size and splendour, and marking time with its blinking orange standby button, Al's 50-inch flat-screen TV waited.

Pontoon

The university year had been finished for a fortnight, but unlike his flatmates, who'd gone home after their last exams, Scott – who was two thirds of the way through an Arts degree – had walked into the city and signed on with a recruitment agency. 'I'll be a graduate soon,' he'd said, when he talked on the phone to his worried parents. 'I have to get a feel for the job market.'

Emptied of flatmates the large house seemed hollow and fragile. A cold wind blew for days on end: windows wobbled in their frames and down the long hallway doors sucked open and shut. One night, fearing an invasion, Scott patrolled from room to room with a cricket stump held down and away from his body like a loaded rifle. Other than a few posters being lifted off their pins there was nothing to report, but lying next to the stump that night he wondered if his decision to stay had been the wrong one.

The next day, though, the storm had passed. Sun shone through the tall windows and the house felt light and airy. He shook his head and laughed at the cricket wicket in the bed, then, with a towel, walked the short distance to the harbour. It was so calm that the surrounding hills, the white mass of a ferry and even the city's dark buildings were perfectly duplicated. He put the towel on the sand and went in. He did front crawl and backstroke. Then he started swimming underwater. He'd take three long breaths and, going off landmarks on the shore, see how far he could get. It was quiet, except if there was something like a truck or an unmuffled car on the harbour road, and between the surface and the sea-floor the blue curtain was cool and endless.

After that, with summer arriving early, he got into a rhythm. He would wake late, go to the harbour and practice his swimming and then walk slowly back to the flat, watching the pohutukawa for their first red blaze. The rest of the day, as the cicadas played, he'd bathe in the sun and read either from a text on nineteenth century Europe or from the tomato box full of women's magazines he'd found under his flatmate's bed.

Then one afternoon a consultant from the recruitment agency called.

'Scott, would you say you're the sort of person who likes to help people?'

It seemed an important question, but before Scott could think through a response she continued, 'We're running a two day testing seminar to find candidates suitable to man the phones at the Emergency Services' 111 call centre. I have to tell you Scott, your name leapt off the page.'

It was early in the morning on day two of the seminar. Unable to sleep, Scott was in the bathroom shaving. At the end of the previous day the recruitment consultant – her long dark hair was styled in a way that suggested she'd travelled to the city in a convertible – stopped Scott outside the lifts and, playing her hands over her cheeks as if applying an exfoliant said, 'Can you guess what I want you to do for me Scott?'

Scott tilted his chin and looked in the mirror. There were spots of blood on his cheek and more on his long neck. It had been his first beard and the shaving had taken less time than he'd expected. Now all that was left was his moustache. He moved his top lip towards his nose and watched the hair bristle forward. After a swim he'd taken to sucking the seawater from it and spitting as he walked out of the water. He turned side on and considered his profile. With his hair damp and neat from the shower he looked like an actor from a pornographic movie.

He shaved the moustache, dried his face and went into his bedroom. It was warm already, but still dark. The numbers on his clock-radio burned in their red, square way. He sat on the edge of the bed feeling his cheeks and chin. They were tight, sore, and as smooth as the belly of a fish. His trousers from the day before were slumped over a chair. Next to the chair, beside the huddled shape of yesterday's shoes, were his swimming shorts.

The previous morning, attending day one of the seminar, Scott had taken a lift to the seventh floor of a tall, grey building in the city. A woman looked up from a computer when he came out of the lift. He hadn't talked to anyone for a few days and when he said his name and what he was there for his voice came out high and weird. The receptionist didn't seem to notice, just made a mark on a piece of paper and then showed him into a room. There were a lot of people at a large table and only a few empty chairs. The table looked like it was set for dining. In front of every person or chair there was a white booklet. On either side of each booklet were a blue pen and a highlighter. At the right-hand corner of the booklet was a glass and in the middle of the table, jugs of water on a white cloth. Though thin, Scott had to get side-on to work down the corridor between the wall and the edge of the table. He sat beside an older man and looked closely at the highlighter. A clock was ticking. Someone sneezed. At the end of the table a policeman said something to a tired looking man. Sitting next to them was the glamorous woman with the dark hair.

The door opened and a short, wide woman walked in. Her hair was gelled back. She started down the opposite side of the table. It was a tight squeeze for her and she became red in the face. 'Excuse me,' she said smiling sadly at the quiet people around the table. Then her handbag hooked on the back of a chair and she was straightened up and held for a moment. 'For God's sake,' her red face shrank as she scrabbled at where the bag was attached. 'Oh . . . hell!' she said, freeing the bag and staring around. The dark-haired woman had half stood up. She was smiling and gesturing with long hands towards an empty chair, but the woman with the fringe was retreating. She was more bullish this time and when she bunted the table a Polynesian man looked around at her and, holding up his glass as if it were in danger, directed a look at the policeman that said, 'Should we arrest her?'

She made it out of the room, but then suddenly returned, jamming her hot wet face around the door. 'Thank you all for your lovely bloody welcome!'

Scott felt the sweat in his underarms. Someone made a sound that could have been a laugh or a cough. The policeman had taken off his hat and was staring into it as if a complicated message were pinned there.

A few minutes later the dark-haired woman stood up and welcomed them. She introduced herself and the men sitting with her, told the candidates about the toilets and what to do if there was an earthquake, then ran through the two-day timetable. After a moment of silence she leaned forward and told them they were about to embark on what could be a life-changing journey. Most of the candidates nodded and smiled. The Polynesian man rubbed his hands together.

'Now,' continued the dark-haired woman, 'so we can get to know you all a little better, I want you to talk to the person next to you and find out three interesting things you can share with the rest of us.' There was a good smell off her – citrus and leather. 'You have five minutes,' she said.

Scott's neighbour was Jeff. Jeff used all the time talking about the conspiracy that had cost him his last job. Scott was interested and was trying to think of a quote from Marx when the dark-haired woman clapped and said, 'Time's up! Let's find out what makes you wonderful people tick.'

Jeff didn't have anything on Scott so when it came to his turn he said, 'This is Scott, he likes . . .' He looked at Scott and put his hands over the table as if waiting to be given a bowl of soup.

'Swimming,' said Scott, 'in the sea.'

The dark-haired woman made a doggy-paddle motion and said, 'Swimming?'

The policeman marked a piece of paper.

'A mermaid with a beard,' said the Polynesian man. He'd brought his own pens and instead of introducing his neighbour had introduced himself, talking passionately about his time in the Territorials. The other candidates liked his mermaid joke. It got about the same amount of laughter as when a woman named Shona introduced her partner. 'This is Lisa. She's an Australian, *but* she's in love with Dan Carter. So she can't be too bad.'

Before morning tea the policeman spoke to a slide show. There were pictures of an ambulance leaving a yellow building, of people wearing head–sets staring intently at computer screens, and a flow-chart describing how the right decision is made. The room had been darkened for the presentation and after the last slide the policeman stood in front of the blue square the projector made on the wall, and, as a white cursor blinked just above his head, told them there was no point in him pussy-footing around, the call centre was a high pressure environment. 'In the next few days we'll be finding out whether you do or don't have the right stuff.'

The room was quiet. Shona said something in a worried voice to the woman beside her.

'Would it be fair to say,' said the dark-haired woman, turning on the lights and looking at the policeman with her hand in a fist under her chin, 'the call centre is a work hard/play hard sort of environment?'

The policeman blinked in a surprised way as if he'd forgotten where he was. 'That might be one way of putting it,' he said after a pause. 'Gary . . .' he tilted his head at the tired looking man.

'We do know how to party,' said Gary, filling his cheeks with breath then shaking his head and releasing the air as if he couldn't begin to start telling them how much and how hard they liked to party. Gary worked at the call centre. After morning tea he talked to them about what he called the nuts and bolts of the job. He told them about the rates of pay, the team leaders, last year's Christmas party, about how there was always a sworn police officer on duty in case things got 'sticky'. And how, as non-sworn police, they had access to affordable holiday homes in Picton and the central North Island.

'Rotovegas,' drawled the Territorial.

On cue everyone, including Scott, looked around at each other and nodding into the middle of the table and at the Territorial, laughed.

Gary smiled and shrugged. 'As far as call centre jobs go,' he said, 'this isn't the worst.'

'Just as far as call centre jobs, Gary?' interrupted the dark-haired woman. 'Or jobs in general?' Then she sat forward as if Gary's answer would determine the fate of the world.

Before the first task of the day they were given time to get a drink and go to the toilet.

'Do we have time for a smoke?' asked a woman wearing a white cardigan.

'I should say no . . .' said the dark-haired woman, looking at the policeman.

'Nicotine slaves,' said the policeman, tugging at his cuffs in a pleased sort of way. 'I gave up last year. Now I run marathons.'

'Fifteen minutes,' said the dark-haired woman.

Scott went with Jeff into the staffroom and filled a plastic cup at the water cooler. Jeff made a hot drink and they sat on a couch and watched a television where men and women were holding metal rings and doing abdominal exercises.

'You know what we should do?' whispered Jeff, peering suspiciously at some of the other candidates who were hovering around the tea and coffee. 'We should form an alliance.'

Scott hadn't known what to say. He'd shaken Jeff's dry old hand.

'A giant meteor is plummeting towards the Earth. There's only time for one spaceship to get to the space station. The spaceship seats eight people. Everyone else on Earth will die. As a group decide which six people from the list will be on the spaceship.' The dark-haired woman raised a pretty finger. 'There are two other spaces you need to fill . . . Select two people from this group to travel into space. The future of the human race is in your hands so choose carefully.'

Using two pens and noises from his mouth the Territorial drummed out the Mission Impossible soundtrack.

The policeman smiled at the iced half of a biscuit he'd been examining.

'It's like *Survivor*,' crowed someone further down Scott's side of the table.

'Are there any questions?' said the dark-haired woman.

'Can we choose you?' smiled the Territorial.

'Do . . .' said Jeff holding up both hands as the laughter faded. 'Do the two people who travel to space have a better chance of getting the job?' Jeff smiled at Scott and then looked back at the dark-haired woman in a way that said, I already know the answer. I'm just getting confirmation for my young friend here.

'It's really an assessment of your communication skills,' said the dark-haired woman. Then raising her hand as if hoping to focus the group and to prevent any more questions, she looked at her watch and said, 'You have twenty minutes. Your time starts now.'

Nobody said anything for a few minutes. Shona coughed and then whispered to Lisa who put her handbag on the table and took out a sachet of tissues.

'Seventeen minutes left,' said the dark-haired woman.

'Some of the people on this list are dead,' said a man in a Bart Simpson tie.

'Just presume they're all alive. It's not real life,' said the dark-haired woman tightly.

'I think I should be on the spaceship,' announced the Territorial.

'Why's that?' said Jeff. 'Are you an astronaut?'

'Should I write his name down?' said Shona, holding a pen over a piece of paper.

'I've got leadership and survival skills,' said the Territorial. 'And, age is on my side.'

Jeff smiled conspiratorially at Scott, picked up the booklet and batted its end against the table as if it were an important sheaf of documents. 'Maybe what we should be talking about,' he said, 'is whether we even want to be on that spaceship.'

'The Russians put a monkey in space,' said the man in the tie.

'Fourteen minutes left,' said the dark-haired woman.

'We'll definitely be taking Princess Di,' said the Territorial.

'Why would we take her?' said Scott.

The clock ticked noisily. Even Jeff looked at Scott in a strange way.

'I suppose you want to lead the mission?' said the Territorial.

Scott had a liquidy feeling in his stomach. 'It's just –'

The policeman had stood up and had gone behind Shona who was writing on the paper. 'Did I do something wrong?' she said, staring up at the policeman.

'You need to start making decisions,' said the dark-haired woman.

'Here,' said the Territorial reaching towards Shona, 'give me the paper.'

After lunch the policeman was all business. He stood with his hands behind his back and spoke in a loud voice. 'The next task is what I call a live fire exercise. We want an idea of how you perform under pressure. You will be taking a mock 111 call.'

The Territorial pumped his fist and said, 'Shot.'

The policeman talked on. 'The person calling you might be upset, or angry, or aggressive. They might be in pain or afraid . . . Gary.' The policeman went over to the window.

Gary stared at something on the far wall. 'They might have locked themselves in the shower and be talking to you while a man with a knife goes through their house.'

There was silence. The dark-haired woman started to say

156

something, but then stopped. The Territorial looked about in an outraged way, then made a face and cracked his neck from one side to the other.

'You have to support this person,' continued the policeman, coming back to the table. 'But at the same time you have to gather information – that means listening.' He tugged at the bottom of his ear.

'Can we work in pairs?' said Shona.

The policeman ignored her. He leaned over the table. 'You are here to assist the caller. Not make friends. Keep your emotions out of it. Stay calm –'

'Breathe,' said Gary.

Jeff had not come back from lunch. No one had said anything about it. Scott looked at the empty chair and then up at Gary. He was talking about a trainee who'd fainted. 'She went bonk,' said Gary, making a falling motion with his arm. 'Straight onto her keyboard.'

Scott was called third. Even though he'd had two cups of water his throat was dry. The dark-haired woman walked with him down a corridor and into a small cool room. There was a desk and an elaborate looking phone with a headset attached by a coiled wire. 'That's the phone,' she said. This close the smell off her was strong, but still good. She put a pen and a piece of paper on the desk. 'You get five minutes to read the instructions. When the phone rings press the button and say, 'What is the emergency?''

'What is the emergency?' said Scott.

'That's right,' said the woman. Her lips glistened and made a sound when they parted.

She left. Scott sat down and put the headset on. The chair swivelled all the way around and went up, down, forward and back. 'This is Mission Control,' he said quietly. He read the instructions twice and underlined some of the information.

Beside the desk there was a rubbish bin with a banana in the bottom. The phone rang. He scratched his beard and looked at the phone. The large red button was glowing softly as though it had got suddenly warm. He pressed it and said what he'd been told to say.

'I'm in a phone box,' said a man doing a woman's voice.

Gary, thought Scott. It sounded like he'd been running. Then, before Scott had time to say anything, the woman started in. There was something about a Valiant and a man in a white hat. Then, for what seemed like half an hour, she did a lot of sobbing and screaming.

At the end of the day each candidate went in front of the panel. A de-brief, the dark-haired woman called it. 'A one-on-one,' said the policeman.

'With chocolate,' countered the dark-haired woman.

Scott was one of the last called. He sat at the end of the big table. You could have played table tennis in the space between them.

'How do you think you went today, Scott?' said the dark-haired woman.

'Scott S.,' said the policeman, looking at a piece of paper and then at Scott as if he'd never seen him before. 'Where do you think you might be in five years?'

Scott didn't know about five years. Since the summer started he'd been thinking about a bag you could swim with. You'd wear a strap across your chest; there'd be a line and then the buoyant, brightly-coloured bag. It would hold your lunch, your shoes, a shirt and tie. It wouldn't just be about fitness or commuting. It was as much about being in the sea – there you felt part of something immense, which made you feel small, but more aware of yourself and therefore somehow big. Scott didn't have it exactly worked out, but he felt close to something crucial.

He cleared his throat and talked about serving somewhere in the government. The enforcement agencies or the Ministry of Justice. 'Helping people do the right thing,' he said.

Gary was bending to pick something off the floor. For a moment it was just his head – his chin on the table and his eyes looking down at Scott. He sat back with a yellow chocolate wrapper.

'I didn't give you your chocolate,' said the dark-haired woman, standing up and gliding down the side of the table.

'Can you hack the call centre?' said the policeman.

The dark-haired woman put two chocolates on the table in front of Scott. 'We liked what we heard,' she said.

'We were impressed,' said the policeman.

Gary yawned and nodded at the others. 'This guy might have what it takes,' he said.

Scott had decided to go for a swim. He was wearing his togs and a sweatshirt and carrying the towel he'd used after shaving. He crossed the road to the footpath overlooking the bay. A grader was shifting a pile of sand from one end of the beach to the other and out on the water a sturdy boat was motoring into the wide bite of the bay towing a pontoon. Scott sat on the low wall which separated the footpath from the sand. The boat stopped. He could hear the voices of the men on board – they wore life jackets and woollen hats and as he watched they fixed the pontoon to a heavy chain, replacing a pink buoy that had been there all winter.

The boat started up, turned and motored slowly away. In the morning light the pontoon's geometry was sharp. Its black, rubbery front was reflected in the still surface of the harbour and it had a shiny ladder and a green surface. Scott walked down to the water. The sand was hard and crenulated where the grader had been. He dropped his towel and went into the cool familiar water. When he went under and started to swim there was the dull sound of the grader and, he thought, the fading whine of the sturdy boat's engine, or perhaps the whine of the city itself. Ahead of him, breaking the blue curtain, was the dark blur of the pontoon. He swam around to the ladder and putting his feet on the cold bottom rung pulled himself out of the water. He climbed the ladder and went across the non-slip surface to the edge of the pontoon. He could see his flat, the narrow road down to the bay, and the road into the city that, as if a tap had been turned on, was suddenly busy with cars, bicycles and − full of faces − a yellow bus. Everyone was going in the same direction, towards the city − where the buildings basked in the golden sun − and wasting no more time Scott dove off the pontoon and swam to shore.

★

Five years later a pod of dolphins stranded themselves on that city beach. The scientists couldn't explain it. It's the heat, one of them said. It's *us*, said another holding her hands just beneath her heart and blushing, something about what we're doing is just not right.

Some of the mammals were saved, cajoled into deeper water by men and women in wet suits and on kayaks. Others died on the sand, the vents in their heads drying open so that the flies could start their work that much faster. Some seemed to have been saved, but it had got into their brains and once they hit the mouth of the harbour, where fast deep currents made rivers between continents, they careened down, down, and then shot back through the surface, making long arcing runs and breathtaking flights before they gave out and fell, tumbling like knotted towels, towards the dark seat of the ocean.

160

Three bikes

Evelyn's allowed me some beer money and I'm drinking in the old part of Oamaru. The pub is at the base of a fork in the road and is one in a block of historic cream- and sand-coloured buildings. The high sun makes dark shadows under their sills and shallow doorways. I sip the beer and then put the glass against my forehead. At the only other table three tourists, two men and a woman, are using a language I don't understand. The woman has long legs. There's a bracelet around her ankle that's white against her dark skin.

A man with a curling moustache and a bowler hat rides past on a penny farthing. The woman stares and says something. The man on the bicycle doffs his hat. A little girl runs by, following the rider as he makes a careful turn, and disappears around the end of the pub. The road down there is narrow. On the sea side there's a bakery and low brick warehouses. The other side (a gallery, an indoor market and a shop that sells stone carvings) is made up of the backs of the buildings that front this street. The tanned woman picks up a bottle of water and follows the two men and the little girl.

Evelyn and I got married and left Dunedin last Friday.

'From now on, it's my way or the highway,' she'd said. And on the way up, once the baby was asleep she had more to say, 'No shift work. No late night drinking. No cell phones.'

The woman who served me comes out, looks at the empty table, and then walks to where she can see down the narrow road. She stands there rolling a cigarette and watching whatever is happening, then shifts the tourists' empty glasses to the side of the table and sits down. As she's about to light her cigarette there's a voice from inside the pub. She holds the flame before the tip of the cigarette and looks intently through the open door. 'Yep, I heard that,' she says. There's a tuft of tobacco at the end of the cigarette. It catches and is consumed as she inhales. She breathes out and looks over, but doesn't say anything. When she's finished she collects up the glasses and the ashtray and goes inside.

I finish the beer and put my hand in my pocket. There's enough for one more.

It's dim inside. Dust slants in sheets where the sun cuts narrow windows. When I arrived there was a big man at the bar with a sandwich. He's still there. The woman is behind the bar, standing as if she and the man have been talking. A motorbike goes by. The woman stares past me and exchanges a shake of the head with the man.

'Same again?' she says, taking my glass. On her finger is a ring in the shape of a crouching cat.

I take my beer outside. The road is wide and so empty you could race elephants.

After a while the man comes out and puts his drink on the other table. He takes little steps as if getting ready to jump from a plane, then puts his hands on his hips and tips back three times. There's a sound out of him when his bend is at its deepest.

'Crook back,' he says, looking over.

I nod and taste my beer. He shifts a chair from the table and sits with his back to me. He lights a cigarette and flicks the match onto the road. A seagull flies down to look.

'Go on,' says the woman, making a move towards the bird. She's come outside with her hand as a shade over her eyes. The bird goes into the middle of the road and tilts its head.

'Wouldn't stop there,' says the man. 'Wouldn't stop there. Not with that Rod about.' Any louder, his voice would echo.

The woman turns towards me and says, 'The sea's just over there.' She nods back to where, beyond the warehouses, there are disused rail lines, a rocky shore, then the ocean. 'Not that you'd know it today.'

'It's hot,' I say.

'Hot as a bastard,' she says, going into the doorway.

'It's good for the pores,' says the man, talking up at the sky. The flesh of his neck creases and bulges.

I sip my beer. Two gulls fly at lamppost height down the road. One of them shits. It spreads and hits the road without a sound.

The only thing moving on the man is his drinking arm.

Three campervans go by.

'Off to see the penguins,' says the man. 'You ever eaten it?'

'Oi,' says the woman, coming into the sun. She slaps the man on his shoulder, and then walks over to my table. Two jade green veins track up the inside of her thigh.

'You're not a tourist,' she says.

'Shifted from Dunedin,' I say.

She spins around in a way that suggests there's been a bet. 'See. Not a tourist.'

The man continues. 'You need a good size drum to poach them properly.'

There is the same motorbike noise. A black three-wheeled

motorcycle comes down the middle of the road. The rider is wearing a visor-less helmet. He has bare arms and wears a gentle look of concentration like a man changing a baby.

'Waaaahhhhhh,' shouts the woman, doing the fingers with both hands.

The big man has stood and shifted the chair back. We watch the bike depart. A chip packet plays in the back-draft.

'He'll come back,' says the woman. 'Just wait.'

The big man steps unsteadily onto the road.

'*Errol*,' says the woman.

He stops halfway across the first lane and braces himself as if preparing for a broken wave.

Far down the road the bike turns. There is blue in the black of its paint job. It catches the sun like the body of a blowfly. There is its roar, the seated shape of the rider, and then it's on us.

'Why don't ya . . .' the big man starts.

But whatever it is is drowned as the bike goes by. The man holds his position; crouched low and squinting with his hands out like it's him on the bike.

The bike revs and changes gear to take the corner. The sound gradually falls.

'Every bloody Saturday,' says the woman. 'Like there's not enough roads round North Otago.'

Still in the middle of the road, the man is marking a long neck-height line with his forefingers. 'One of those trip wires the Indians use,' he says, 'that would do it. Take his head clean off.'

'Then what?' says the woman as if considering it. 'We've got a rider-less bike blatting about?'

'The headless horseman,' says the man, doing his back exercises. He comes off the road and sits down.

The woman goes back to the doorway. The hot quiet resumes.

'You want another?' says the woman as I finish my beer.

I shake my head. 'No thanks.'

'He's a family man,' says the man. 'He can't spend all day here.'

'How would you know?' says the woman. 'How do you know he's not like you?'

'I saw the ring on his finger.'

She crosses her arms over her small breasts.

'I got married on Friday,' I say.

'Friday?' bellows the man. 'Friday gone?'

There's a distressed female voice out on the road.

'Here's his Missus now,' he says. 'Here for her honeymoon.'

A tandem bicycle comes around the corner. A bright pannier bag is fixed over the front wheel. Three plastic water bottles are attached to different parts of the frame. The woman is on the back. 'Please Marty,' she says, 'just for one damn day.'

The man's wearing broad tinted glasses and a cobalt helmet.

'Marty?' says the woman.

The man doesn't say anything. As they go past the pub the woman lifts her feet off the pedals and starts shaking from side to side.

'God damn it!' says the man still pedalling.

They wobble this way and that down the street.

'Yeah!' says the barwoman. 'Let the bastard have it.'

The man manages to keep the bike upright. 'What did I say about wobbling!' he shouts.

The woman stops her wobbling, but keeps her toes pointed to the heavens. Her pedals revolve uselessly.

I stand and for some reason do the same stretch as the big man.

'There's a band on tonight.' He's turned to watch the cyclists, his stomach peeks around the side of the chair.

'Yeah?' I say.

'From Timaru.'

'Radio's saying it's thirty-three degrees,' says the woman, 'and they reckon it's going to get hotter.'

'Well,' I say, raising my hand and going out onto the road. There is the sound of a car. It's Evelyn. I stop and watch her come in. A black plastic shade is stuck to the back window. Driving helps the baby sleep.

I go around the front of the car and quietly get into the front seat.

'So?' says Evelyn in her way.

We've fixed mirrors to the back of the passenger seat so we can check our daughter. I go to shift the rear-vision mirror, but Evelyn grabs it. With her other hand she takes my wrist.

'No,' she says. And then, 'You'll break it.'

But I keep at it and eventually she lets go. I look at our daughter. Every time we talk about a name an argument starts up.

'New friends?' says Evelyn eventually.

They haven't moved out there. The man says something. The woman's mouth moves in return and she disappears inside. The man looks over at the car and, very deliberately, raises his empty glass.

Soup

The pools were like big steel sinks. Underground water came through vents in the bottom of each pool. The pool the brothers were in was warm and rectangular. The hot one was round. They held about the same amount of water. The plunge pool was also made of steel though it was smaller and deeper. More like a well, thought Ryan. He doubted he'd go in, but when he said that Dirk laughed. 'Wait until we've tried the hot one,' he said.

Ryan had been staying with Dirk in Gisborne for the past three days. His relationship with Ann had collapsed. She'd said she didn't understand him. She'd said other things too. Ryan called Dirk from a bus station in Auckland. 'Stay as long as you need,' Dirk said.

It had rained every day since Ryan arrived. That morning had been no different.

'Cabin fever,' Dirk had said, looking around their small flat at the boxes and drawers overflowing with brand new nappies and undersized linen. 'Let's go down to the hot pools.'

'I'll do some baking,' Michelle said.

'You won't come?'

Michelle touched her tummy then smiled and put a hand on Dirk's hip.

'How will we dress a poached baby?'

Dirk made a shallow bow. 'It's you and me then, Ryan.'

Ryan nodded. He'd been at the dining table thinking about writing Ann a letter.

The high, sloping roof over the pools was the shape of a sail. The changing sheds and a wall of cubby holes blocked one end and one side of the pools. The rest was fenced off. Through the fence there was a strip of grey sky and some bush. Dirk said that the stream that fed the plunge pool was down there as well. There were little spools of slime in the water. Dirk made scissors with his fingers and tried to snare them.

'Like Mr Miyagi,' he said, 'trying to catch flies.'

It had been their favourite movie when they were young, but Ryan gave up after one go and went back to thinking about Ann.

Dirk's cellphone beeped and vibrated pool-side. Michelle had made him put it in a glad-bag and she'd also given them some biscuits and fruit for the drive. Ryan's cellphone was in Rotorua. The bus from Auckland had stopped there and Ryan had taken the phone into a public toilet. When Ann answered he put the phone into the urinal and started pissing. It made him feel better. But by the time the bus left Rotorua he was crying again.

'Mum can't wait to be a grandma,' Dirk said, holding up the phone in the bag.

They climbed out. Ryan pointed to the plunge pool and they went over to look. Ryan was reluctant.

'It'll be good for you,' said Dirk. He had his arms crossed and they looked strong. Ryan compared them to his own that were thin and hairy and added another reason for Ann forcing him from their flat. Those thoughts disappeared

168

when he dipped his foot into the plunge pool. 'No bloody way,' he said. But Dirk was between him and the other pools and Ryan knew his brother's next move so he went cautiously down the stairs. The water stopped at his chest.

'There you go,' Dirk smiled, 'now try the rest.'

When Ryan came up he was huffing and shooting water out of his face. He looked at Dirk and smiled.

Dirk took a turn in the cold water and then they got into the hot pool. They talked about how their skin was tingling and then both made satisfied sounds and leaned back so only their faces broke the surface. It was nice for a moment, but then the hot buzzing underwater sound started Ryan thinking about Ann's birthday at a Mexican restaurant the year before. He sat up like someone in the movies waking from a nightmare. Dirk watched Ryan for a while and then he too sat up. He told Ryan about the last time he and Michelle had been there. The track from the carpark climbed past the pools to a look-out with a view over Mahia, the peninsula, and Poverty Bay. They were not far from the look-out when they heard a clattering above them. It sounded as if something terrible was coming down the track.

'My first thought was a bear,' said Dirk. 'I know that's stupid, but it reminded me of that time in Canada. Next thing, this herd of goats are stampeding towards us. There were so many of them and going so fast it was like they'd been shot out of a goat-gun. I jumped, grabbed a branch, and hung like a monkey. Michelle just stood there and the goats charged down either side of her.' Dirk looked at the phone in the plastic bag. 'That was a few weeks before she got pregnant.'

'Maybe they were magic goats,' said Ryan.

They heard voices and footsteps on the gravel track outside the pools. The doors into the changing sheds slammed and there was silence. Dirk was asking Ryan a question about a rugby game they'd watched on television the night before when the changing shed door opened and an enormous Maori man in a mustard coloured singlet and Stubbie shorts walked out of the shed and around the edge of the hot pool. He had a handful of clothes, a packet of chips, sachets of Raro, and a large empty plastic bottle. His fleshy ears were the length of a man's hand.

'Aotea?' he called, looking back at the sheds.

There was a response but no clear words and he left his gear in the cubby holes and stepped carefully down the stairs into the hot pool. The level of the pool went up. In the middle of the pool he made a shovel of his hands and doused his huge head and face with the hot water. He smiled. He didn't have many teeth.

'Good day for it,' said Dirk.

The large man was watching over the brothers' heads. A tiny girl in a black and purple bathing suit darted out of the women's changing shed. She had an armful of clothes and was running on the sides of her feet.

'You want to come in here?' said the large man.

The girl shook her head and after dropping off her clothes and shoes went into the warm pool and submerged herself so that the water was at her chin.

'Chips?' said the large man.

'No thanks,' said the girl.

'My niece,' said the large man. 'We're always up here.'

'It's good here,' said Dirk.

Ryan nodded and pushed his hand through the water. Coils of slime spiralled and somersaulted.

'Where are you from?' said Dirk.

'Mahia,' said the large man. 'I drive the school bus.'

Dirk's face was red and there was sweat on his forehead. He got onto the side of the pool leaving his legs in the water. In the other pool the little girl was going around with the water just below her eye level. There was a sign on the wall that said not to go under. WATERBORNE MENINGITIS, it said.

'Where you fellas from?' said the large man. He looked at Ryan but Dirk answered.

'Gisborne, my brother's from Auckland.'

'Oh,' said the large man. 'I'm sorry to hear that.' His laughter shook the fat over his body and there were little waves across the pool. The brothers laughed. Dirk put his hand over his forehead and through his hair then stood up and walked to the plunge pool. When he was about to step in the large man said in a serious voice, 'Wouldn't go in there.'

Dirk turned around. 'Why not?' he said, his smile fading.

'Because of the Taniwha,' said the little girl.

The way a bird would talk, thought Ryan. She and the large man laughed.

'Every time there's a new person, eh Aotea?'

The little girl was back to submarining around the pool. Her eyes smiled at the large man.

Ryan and the large man watched Dirk in the cold water. He went under a few times and, like the large man had done, splashed the cold water over his face. Then he looked out to where the bush was being knocked around by the wind and rain.

'He likes it here eh?' said the large man.

Ryan nodded. 'He's waiting to be a father.' He pointed a dripping finger at the phone by the pool.

Dirk came back to the hot pool. His skin was red. 'Pfoar Jesus,' he said, flicking water from his hair at Ryan.

'Get out of it,' said Ryan.

Dirk got into the water and onto his knees so that the water covered his shoulders. The large man's feet were like clubs. They were making circling motions and above them the water on the surface was whirling around itself. Ryan started to feel too hot. He could feel the pulse in his neck. He went into the plunge pool and the pockets of his shorts puffed out to the side like ears. Ann had gone into the bathroom after she told him to leave. He'd tried to get the door open. 'I'm not coming out,' she'd said, 'not until you go.' He'd heard the bath plug tinkle on its chain and then the taps turn on.

There were more footsteps on the path and then like the last time the shed's doors slammed.

Ryan thought about a bikini she'd worn last year. It was blue and white and after modelling it for him she'd held him close. 'I can't go around denying it,' she'd whispered. 'I *am* an Aucklander.'

There was a pattering sound. Another little girl was skipping around the side of the pools. She was carrying a pink bag. Shoes and clothes were sticking out of it and when she got into the warm pool she put her arm around the other girl. She was followed by a man with a thin face and T-shirt tan lines.

'Hey bro,' said the large man.

The thin-faced man threw a Pak 'n Save bag of clothes in the direction of the cubby holes. He put his hand on the large man's shoulder as he got into the pool. He looked at Dirk and then Ryan who was still in the plunge pool.

'You getting out of there sometime?' said Dirk.

Ryan's legs and feet were going numb. He climbed out and sat next to his brother pushing against him with his shoulder.

'Strewth,' said Dirk, pushing back at Ryan and picking up the phone.

'Check that out.' The large man lifted his foot out of the water and pointed at the phone in the bag. 'These fellas are from NASA.'

The thin-faced man smiled. He had his arms on the side

of the pool. The rest of him hung down. With his patchy beard he looked like Jesus.

'Did you get that dog?' said the large man.

'Yesterday,' said the thin-faced man.

There was a gust of wind and the bush shook like something was coming through it. The thin-faced man's plastic bag slid across the concrete. The girls in the pool swivelled to watch.

'This guy's a fisherman,' said the large man.

'Oh yeah,' said Dirk. Dirk liked to fish. 'Where do you do that?'

'Out of Tolaga,' said the fisherman. He sniffed at his fingertips and looked at Ryan. His eyes were a cold, washed-out blue.

The large man started telling them about being a Maori Warden. 'We do the pubs in Mahia during the week. In the weekends we come up your way.'

'Do you enjoy it?' said Dirk, then later, 'Do you have any problems with the gangs?'

'Nah, bro, I don't like violence. Anyway, most of those guys are my cousins.'

Ryan was taking his pulse under the water. It seemed fast but he didn't have a watch. The girls were laughing quietly. It was still raining. I wonder what she's doing right now, he thought.

'Yeah, we do Gisborne on Friday and Saturday nights,' said the large man. 'The cops bought us a van, torches and walkie talkies, but they don't pay for our KFC.'

The brothers laughed. The fisherman smiled and looked over at the girls.

The large man went into the middle of the pool and shovelled more water on his face. He turned with his back to the brothers. There were volcanic splotches on his shoulders and back. The fisherman shifted so he was hidden by the large man. 'We got some more of those mushrooms,' he said quietly. 'We were off our heads. My sister ended up chasing the dogs round and round the fucking house. It got dark and she was still doing it.'

'Jean?' said the larger man.

'No,' said the fisherman. 'Paula. No one knows where Jean is.'

The large man turned around and sat beside the fisherman. The two men looked into the middle of the pool.

There was the crunching sound of footsteps on the track outside and a woman talking. She sounded surprised at something.

'What do you reckon?' said Ryan.

Dirk shrugged and stood up. 'No rush is there? You got somewhere you need to be?'

On the drive to the pools Dirk had turned down the stereo. 'Like I said, Michelle and I are happy for you to stay as long as you like. And I know at the moment you probably don't want to talk too much about it –'

Ryan had started to say something but his brother kept talking.

'All I'm saying is if you want to talk, then . . . ' He'd held his hand flat like he was waiting for money or congratulations. Ryan hadn't known what to say. He'd looked at a cow in a paddock. Dirk had waited for a moment then glanced over.

'Okay,' said Ryan. 'Yeah, thanks.'

Dirk had cranked up the music.

'I got hangi waiting for me when I get home,' said the large man. 'Pork, kumara, spuds, chicken.' He counted the ends of his fingers.

'Parsnip, pumpkin,' said the girl from the pool.

'Parsnip, parsnip, parsnip,' said the other girl.

There was a noise from the changing sheds. 'Oh,' a man said, 'my sock.'

'But KFC,' said the large man. 'We get a bucket before work and another one when we finish. The boss complains that we stink out the van. Clean out them fucking chicken bones.' The large man pointed his finger forward and back and wobbled his head side to side. One of his longer teeth got between his lips. One girl and then the other put their hands near their armpits and flapped at the water.

They all laughed.

A man with skin like chalk came through the door of the changing sheds. He had black-rimmed glasses like the newsreaders wear. His hair was neat and his red shorts looked brand new. There was a criss-crossing black tattoo on his upper arm. An accountant, thought Ryan.

'Which is the hot one?' he said, looking at the men in the pool.

'That one,' said the large man, pointing at where Dirk was getting out of the plunge pool.

'This one's the warm one – that one's the hot one – that one's the cold one,' sang the girls. The lighter skinned girl bit into a Cookie-time biscuit. Crumbs from it fell in the pool.

The accountant got into the warm pool. The girls went to the side opposite and twirled each other's hair. There was the noise of a door closing.

'Andrew, Andrew,' said a young Asian woman, 'where do I put my clothes?' Her black hair was a wavy mane down her back. She was wearing a bikini top and her short white shorts fitted her well. The men in the bath watched as she crossed to where Andrew was sitting.

'In there?' she said, looking at the cubby holes. 'What about lockers?'

The fisherman had pulled himself upright. In profile he was handsome and reptilian. Ryan expected a flickering tongue to lap around his mouth.

Dirk's phone rang and shifted about on the wet concrete.

'Incoming,' said the large man. He made the sound of a bomb falling and exploding. Dirk answered the phone. Andrew wet his hand and spiked up his hair. The girls were holding the side of the pool and giggling as the large man made more bombs. The fisherman stared as the Asian girl stepped carefully into the pool. Ryan looked at his brother.

'She's making a chocolate cake,' Dirk said, holding his hand over the end of the phone.

The large man got out of the hot pool. The singlet hung around his knees and his breasts were like bags of milk. He went down the steps into the plunge pool. 'Aah,' he said. The water dripped off his chin and nose. He submerged himself and then stood up. He made a blowing sound. 'Aah,' he said. He was a like a statue in the rain.

'We want Raro,' sung the girls.

The large man nodded. He got out of the pool and went away with some cigarettes, the plastic bottle, and the sachets.

Andrew was out of the warm water and by the hot pool. He put his foot into the hot water and looked over at the Asian woman. 'Way hotter,' he said. But she wasn't watching. She was making popping sounds with her finger on the inside of her cheek. The girls were laughing and so was the fisherman. He had one leg up on the side of the pool.

'She can't find the cocoa,' said Dirk.

Nobody said anything for a while. The Asian woman was turning her hair into a ball on top of her head. Ryan could hear the taps going in the changing room. The large man came out. He cradled the bottle like it was a baby and was rocking the orange fluid back and forward. He gave the bottle to the girl who had come with the fisherman.

'Don't drink it all,' he said, 'save some for me and your dad.' He got back into the hot pool. 'Cold out there,' he said.

The fisherman opened his eyes. 'Cold as a penguin's snatch,' he said slowly.

Ryan was on the side of the pool looking at the hair on his legs. It was moving this way and that.

There was an animal sound from the trees. It was like someone filing a road sign. The two girls said something to each other in excited voices and then ran to the fence and held it like there were zoo animals. Dirk turned around, shifting the cellphone away so he didn't drip onto it. Andrew stood up.

'Candice,' he said, looking over at the Asian woman.

'That's our possum,' said the large man. 'He usually starts around lunch time. Must have slept in today.'

The noise stopped and then started. The fisherman was looking at Candice. She was still ravelling her hair. The under parts of her arms were smooth and white. The noise from the animal got louder like it was seeking something to shatter. Candice looked at the fisherman. Water dripped from his beard. He shaped her name with his mouth. She smiled like a model on a toothpaste advertisement and then went side on and looked at him over her shoulder. The noise stopped and the girls ran back to their pool. Each footfall was like a little clod on the concrete. Bubbles came up through the water by the larger man. 'Pardie,' he said. Then he looked at Ryan. 'If you two are brothers then you're going to be an uncle too.'

Ryan nodded. He wanted to watch Candice.

'He knows that,' said Dirk. 'He knows that's coming.'

The fisherman smiled and then closed his eyes.

Candice had stepped out of the warm pool and was standing by the cubby holes. When she reached for her bag the muscles in the backs of legs went taut like she was wearing high-heeled shoes.

Thinking about stopping

Gary wiped down the last table, checked the lock on the front door, took a beer from the fridge behind the bar, walked across the dining room, through the swing door, through the clean and now quiet kitchen, and out the back door to where Lee and Bruce were sitting on upturned milk crates. Lee gestured at the crate Gary used when they were waiting for service. Gary shook his head. 'Gotta get home,' he said, opening his beer and drinking most of it off.

'Pussy,' said Lee.

'It's his missus,' Bruce said, still in his apron and the boat-shaped hat he claimed kept the sweat out of his eyes. 'She has her needs.'

'And what would *you* know about that?' said Lee.

Bruce straightened his big body and smiled in a way that suggested though he knew plenty, he wouldn't be sharing any secrets tonight.

'Rick's away for a few days,' Lee said, looking back at Gary. 'I've got his truck and dogs.'

Bruce finished his beer and stood. Then, as if a pole

driven into the concrete was also temporarily embedded in his forehead, he walked a tight circle.

'We should call IHC,' said Lee, watching Bruce finish his rotation.

Bruce screwed the lid off another beer and sat down. 'You won't be catching me in any forest.'

Gary smiled. 'But Bruce, we'd be looking for pigs.'

'Yeah Bruce, and anyway, who says you're invited?' said Lee.

Gary put down his empty. 'Right,' he said.

'The morning,' said Lee.

Gary made an ambiguous gesture and started up the narrow road that accessed the rear of the restaurant, a Chinese takeaway, a store that sold the paua-shell teaspoons and stuffed kiwis the tourists went for, and the real estate agency above which he lived with Tania. He'd been working at a bar in Queenstown when they met. Jailbait, Bruce crowed the afternoon they'd watched her walk past the restaurant. It wasn't that bad, but she was young: friends with the earth, honest, and game in bed, with a new thing for comments that suggested she believed, one hundred percent, in the sustainability of their relationship.

The week she'd been offered a job guiding on the Milford Track there'd been some trouble at the bar. A skinhead had come in as Gary was trying to close. He'd smashed a carafe and pissed on the fire. Gary had lost it, booting the man in the balls before dragging him out of the bar and onto the road. The next day three men in a Cortina were parked outside Gary's flat. Despite all the women, Gary had never had a handle on love – what he'd always had a handle on was when to get out of town.

He went up the external stairway and quietly through the door. Tania was in her underwear on top of the bed – her black hair like ink across the pillow. On the bench, beside the little sink, there was a fan of notes: yen and a few US dollars. She liked him to bank their tips every day and, so she could trace the rise in their fortunes, to get a printout of their savings account at the end of the week. It suited Gary. Having a lot of cash around had never been a good idea.

He folded his apron over a chair and took off his T-shirt, shorts, and sports shoes. It was just him and the boss at the front of house. Waiting tables, doing the bar, making coffee. It was as much an endurance event as a job. Not that he minded – he'd always worked hard, but always in cities, in places he could relax after a shift. Pills, pubs, clubs, weed, and acid – Gary was serious about partying. Age hadn't changed that; he'd never expected it to. But Te Anau was for lone Italians and their ten-speeds in tents by the lake, Taiwanese on buses for Milford Sound, Americans in loud, matching belly-bags. For Gary its cupboards were bare: nowhere to party, no one to party with. Tania would have a spliff and some wine with him on her day off, but she was always tired and the more they saved, and the more realistic buying a house-bus appeared, the hornier for money she became.

He sat on the bed. Her tanned shoulders showed the placement of the straps on the pack she carried. Her thighs, where he rested his hand, showed even clearer lines; up to her groin was milk-white and downy. She smiled and said something low, then, still smiling, rolled away from him. Gary reached under the bed for the canister of pills. He put one in his mouth and went to the sink where he swallowed it with a handful of water. Back at the bed he lay down beside her. There was the ceiling, the warm air in the gap between the ceiling and the iron roof, the iron roof, and above that, punched out with planets, moons and stars, hooding quiet old Eastern Southland, the night sky. Down the road Lee started singing Bruce the Warehouse jingle. Then there were those two.

Lee was one of the rare cooks who calmed under pressure. Afterwards though, especially when he was drinking, he'd ride Bruce hard. His favourite angle was to tell him to go back to Invercargill – that he knew people at the Warehouse or Pak 'n Save who could get him a job. Gary had stayed back at the end of a few shifts, but it was all Lee doing variations on that stupid jingle or Lee gooning, mimicking the people who push the trolley-trains around the supermarket carparks. Bruce never gave much back. At his most animated he might shout, 'No, Lee. No, you're wrong about that,' but mostly he'd laugh a short unhappy laugh – Gary heard it now as he closed his eyes – make his all-knowing face and, no matter how drunk, do his little rotation between beers.

Gary woke as Tania left the room. There were her footsteps on the metal stairs and then the fading sound of them on the access road. A bus used its airbrakes. A tourist plane or helicopter flew over. Then there was quiet. Gary got out of bed, went to the window, and split the curtain. Now she was on the pavement beside the main road – walking briskly with her usual bounce, as if about to start skipping. There was a shop awning and she disappeared. He let go of the curtain. Under the sink, at the bottom of a soup pot, there was a pencil case. In the case there were cigarette papers, a pipe, a lighter, and a half full coin-bag of buds. In a corner of the coin-bag there was a neatly folded cigarette paper – inside was his last tab of acid. He fished it out and put it on the sink next to the foreign dollars and the ATM card for the house-bus account. He wet the gum on the cigarette paper and looked at the card, then, before lying on the bed and lighting the joint, he stashed the card and acid in his wallet.

Lee had asked him hunting one other time. It was the week after Gary started at the restaurant and, other than don't fuck with my kitchen old man, the invitation was the first thing said between them. They'd driven out towards Mossburn with Lee's dog in the back. It was fawn with a pink nose and, despite being the animal's first hunt, Lee had high hopes – mightn't look like it, he'd mumbled, but he's got a mean streak. After that Lee talked about his trip to the Gold Coast at the end of the tourist season (Coronas by the pool, wet titty contests), then, as they'd turned down a long forestry road and after Gary lit a thin joint, Lee had really opened up, telling Gary about his and his brother's hunting successes, about his brother's dogs (killing machines), about one dog in particular (the top dog, Ken), that by a bloody miracle had survived a ten-metre fall when the boar it had by the ear went off a cliff, and that since then always ate the bailed pig's back door – if you don't get there fast enough it'll look like the pig's been sat in a food processor.

They'd cut Lee's dog loose and watched as it went into the forest, not as if it were a hunting machine, but as if it were a visitor to a new town, a town which posed no threat and was best appreciated at an amble, the sort of town about which a man would say, I could stay and put down some roots. Here, I could really make a fresh start.

One hour passed and then another. Nothing happened. Lee started playing with a tomahawk, throwing it with two hands at the trees and making war with his hand over his mouth. Gary made a pillow of his jersey and found a place beside the road. Stared at through the gaps in his fingers the tips of the young pines seemed embedded in the sky. He'd woken up when the dog came back. It had narrow eyes and a pregnant belly. 'Bloody thing's been eating possums,' Lee said, grabbing the animal by the collar and looking at Gary as if the hunt's failure were his fault.

. . .

The second hunt, however, was already going differently. This time, despite what Lee had said the night before, Bruce was there, waiting on the road out of town with a rugby sock filled with oranges. 'For half-time,' he'd said, squeezing into the back of the truck.

'Freak,' said Lee, and then, 'Hurry up.' Aside from that, Lee had been quiet for the rest of the drive, busying himself with the stereo, the air-conditioning, the placement of the rear-vision mirror – as if instead of his brother's truck he was piloting an assault helicopter.

Enjoying the quiet, Gary spent the drive watching the white line trace down the state highway, thinking first of the red thread implanted in Band-Aids, then, as he smelt Bruce's oranges, of a Goan morning: two woman – short bare arms, white aprons and thick, black hair made into buns on their heads – had entered his room with sweet tea and cut fruit, and while he'd eaten, staring out across the Arabian sea, they'd made his bed, snapping starched sheets and communicating with each other in the gentle way of birds just before dawn.

And unlike that first hunt, as soon they turned onto the forestry road, the dogs (there were three, including the ashy, broad-jawed Ken) started whining and then barking and then banging into their cages, so that all three men stared out at the forest that was Christmas-tree-green.

Lee stopped the truck and they got out. 'Watch yourselves,' he said, when he opened the cage doors.

The dogs – mouths suddenly serene – went like hell off the truck and down the road, then, at different intervals, and like a search party, they threaded the forest.

Gary climbed onto the bed of the truck and tried to watch, but the trees were recently pruned and the rows between them were clotted with drifts of branches. He took out his wallet and looked for the acid, and, as he did, the dogs' barking, which had started as scattered and deep, shifted – as if now the dogs were all together aboard a scooter – to frantic and focussed.

'They're on to something,' said Lee.

Forgetting the acid, Gary got down from the truck and started towards the forest. 'Wait on, they haven't bailed it yet,' said Lee in the calm manner he used when orders were piling up.

Gary stopped and the three of them stood together and listened. Nearby there was the ticking sound of the truck's cooling engine, while from the forest the barking started to echo, as if whatever deal was going down was going down in a squash court or a bike-shed. Lee tipped forward on his toes. Bruce changed the fruit from one hand to the other causing the hooped sock to pendulate. Then to seal it – in a short break in the barking – there came a rapid panic of squeals.

Lee nodded at the forest. 'That's it,' he said, and off he went.

Gary followed. Making an alley between the trees, there was a downward section of clear ground, a flattening, and then a drift of branches. Lee ran across to the next row and disappeared, while, with head back and limbs pumping, Gary went straight down. His feet jarred as he hit the flat section, but it didn't cost him much and he arrived at the first drift with good speed. He went over in an equine leap with his arms forward and his legs back, landing, sliding, and rotating on a canopy of small branches and needles, so that he was again able to notice the way the tips of the trees appeared to be embedded in the sky, but with the barking a little louder this was no time for noticing, and he righted himself and bounded at and then hurdled another drift, a lower one, and onto even steeper ground (it was more like falling than running) he landed in, rather than went over, the next drift that was deep and broad, like a pool maybe, or a web, like a web of long, thin, needly branches, and the only way to go was to activate all his large as well as small muscle groups, swimming, jiving and flailing as if he were aboard some fitness or martial arts machine that consisted of phalanx after phalanx of obstacles coming at all angles and on all planes, and out of that drift there was a section of uphill and while he scaled that – shooting his arms like the Bionic man – he heard behind him a crashing sound he presumed was Bruce, and then, ahead, there was another drift and this time he made a sweeping turn on the periphery thinking maybe there'd be a passage, but there was none, just dense green and loggy brown and so he veered, as if attached to the dogs' even louder barking, into the drift, and again he was up to his neck in foliage – under other circumstances he might have stopped and enjoyed the coolness and the piney smell and the sighing wind – but he didn't stop, he went up as if climbing a ladder, then after a dive and a roll he was out the other side and accounting for another downward section, then a flat section, and then another section of steep uphill where he really started to feel buggered, and he made a weak scissor kick and a half-hearted barrel roll so that in the next drift he ended wrong way up and, at first, high on the cut branches, then, like a drip on the windscreen, he dribbled into the guts of the drift and stopped.

His eyes gently bulged and blood ran to his face. A brushy sort of branch wagged between his legs. He heard Bruce approaching, huffing and sneezing, as if he'd inhaled something juicy. It was enough for Gary to give it hell one more time, and turning his lower body into an eggbeater and then an outboard motor he got himself down through the branches, onto the earth that was cool and damp, and then through the woody barricade and into open ground where there was another uphill section, and a different barking (it was nearer but thinner, as if more than one of the dogs had found something else to do) and ahead the living forest changed into a stand of dead trees that were like witches' hands and that made a swathe atop a verge, a dead forest and verge that Gary went through and up without stopping, without thinking about stopping, and where, once he got to the top, prickled, sweaty and breathing in tattered, heart pounding gasps, he finally got a view of the action.

The dogs and the brown pig were in what resembled an overgrown skateboarding bowl – sloping walls of rock and, punctuated with flattened or broken witch's hands, a mud floor. The pig was big – had all three dogs been strapped together it would still have been bigger. It had its face against one of the rock walls. One of its legs was shaped in a strange way as if broken while the other kicked back at Ken who was hitting into the pig's rear in the way of a spring lamb. The other dogs were nipping at the face, barking, and zipping from one side of the animal to the other as if seeking their own entrance point.

'Jesus Christ,' said Bruce, coming up beside Gary. He sneezed once and then twice. 'Hay fever –' he started to say.

'Look,' said Gary.

Lee was on the other side of the sump. He had a knife. 'Get out of it Ken,' he shouted, scrambling down the rocks.

Ken stayed put – all you could see was his ash-coloured rear and the exclamation mark his short stiff tail made with his arsehole – but the other dogs retreated. Lee shouted again and this time Ken drew out of the pig and looked. His head and neck were crimson. 'Ken,' roared Lee. Ken went away from the back of the pig and around to the front where he grabbed onto the pig's ear and pulled. The pig listed like a torpedoed ship. Lee straddled its back, held the snout, and made an arc around its neck. Ken ducked into the blood.

The smallest dog whined. Bruce sneezed. A fantail zagged over the sump.

'Who's carrying?' said Lee, after a moment.

Back at the truck Lee took out a bottle of Southern Comfort. 'A pig like that,' he said, 'you have to have a drink.'

The gutted pig was on the bed of the truck. The well fed dogs were asleep in the cages. Bruce and Gary were prone on the grass, angled off each other like cheeses on a board. Lee had said he didn't want the pig. He had enough pork at home to feed the marine corp. Gary wasn't interested either. Tania stuck to fish and the freezer in their room was the size of a microwave. But Bruce was keen – pork sausages, chops, pot roasts, steaks, bacon, back straps, pork loin – you beauty. Lee showed him how to wear the pig – fixing the forelegs like straps over his shoulders – and they'd headed off. Beyond the dead forest Bruce said he was rooted and Gary took over. The legs were bristled and baskety – they seemed too thin for the body – while the head slapped heavily against his head like the lid of a rubbish skip. The distance they could carry the pig got shorter and shorter. Lee didn't help. Your pig, your carry, he said, holding a stick at his shoulder. The uphill sections were runways. The drifts were themselves forests; they were Olympic-length swimming pools. The pig bled into the waists and then the seats of their trousers – it bled down the back of their knees and ringed the tops of their socks. It grew heavier and heavier and they heaved and swore and held each other under the arms and by the forearms, pulling, pushing and righting each other when they fell. They cheered each other step by step, 'A little further, that's it mate, you can do it, drop it there, my turn, my turn, good shit.'

Bent in half Bruce sneezed glugs of snot, while when it

was his turn Gary was made deaf by the whoosh and bang of his heart.

'Thank fuck,' 'Shit fucking hot,' they cried when they saw the truck, and after swinging the carcass aboard they fell together into the grass.

Bruce was still breathing too hard to take a drink, but Gary sat up and had a go. It was warm and sweet and he followed his first gulp with another two.

'Good carry,' said Lee, taking the bottle.

Bruce sneezed. His big body shot up and then slumped as if touched by resuscitation paddles.

'He's allergic to exercise,' said Lee.

Bruce sneezed again and this time sat up. Still panting, he spat and cleared his nostrils into the grass. He held his hand at the bottle.

'What do you say?' said Lee.

Bruce snuffled. 'C'mon,' he said.

Lee kept the bottle just out of his reach. Bruce got to his knees and made a lunge, but Lee whipped it away. 'You know what?' he said, as if he'd just had a great idea. 'I'd love a piece of orange.'

Bruce still had his hand at the bottle. 'C'mon,' he said again.

With a flourish Lee offered and then removed the bottle. 'Like at rugby, when the coach's missus brought out a bag of segments.'

Bruce sneezed.

'Where are those oranges?' said Lee.

Gary lay back so as to get the wallet out of his pants. It had wilted with the sweat.

'Hmm?' said Lee, as if talking to a child. He unscrewed the lid, drank, and sighed with the joy of it. Glancing at Gary he pointed the bottle at Bruce as if it were a sword.

'Did you lose them up your fat arse?'

The folded paper and the acid inside were still intact.

'Hey Gary,' said Lee, 'wouldn't you like an orange?'

Gary cast his eyes at Bruce and then back to Lee. He put his finger to his lips, raised his eyebrows and showed Lee the square of acid.

Lee pushed off the truck and went over. He turned his back to Bruce. 'Acid?' he whispered.

'It's a smooth ride,' said Gary.

'I knew it,' said Lee. 'I knew you were on something.'

'Put it on your tongue.'

Lee wet his finger, dipped it, and put it in his mouth.

The bank, where Gary and Bruce lay, was in sunshine. The truck was in shade. Lee was still changing tyres. The bottle was mostly empty. Bruce was talking about the time he'd lived in Christchurch. 'Worked in a chip shop in Woolston,' he said.

Gary held the ATM card so that there was just it and the sky. Tania's name was raised off the plastic. There were three thousand and ninety-eight dollars in the account.

Bruce's face was red from the alcohol, but the sneezing had stopped. Blood dried in the creases of his gut. He picked at the hair there. 'You think *it* gets busy,' he waved back across the forests, farm land and subdivisions to the waiting restaurant. 'Four deep fryers going full bore, orders all the way to Africa, drunks scrapping out the front.' He counted the challenges on his fingers.

There was the now familiar sound of lug nuts being tightened and then the sound of the jack. The truck lowered. Lee appeared at the front of the truck holding a tyre iron.

Gary sipped from the bottle. 'Your slowest yet,' he said, putting the card back in his wallet.

'What? Bullshit.'

Gary shrugged, suggesting time was beyond his control.

Lee spat drily then went back to the other side of the truck and returned with the jack. 'Again,' he said.

Gary raised his arm. Lee slid the jack under the truck and looked over his shoulder. Gary dropped his arm. Lee pumped furiously. The truck tilted causing the pig to shift gently. Gary settled in the grass. 'We'll let him do one more,' he said.

'On weekends we'd go and give the Wizard a hard time,' said Bruce.

A plane moved slowly across the sky. This time tomorrow, thought Gary, I could be in Adelaide.

Lee rolled a wheel down the side of the truck. He knocked it off its balance and it toiled with gravity while he went back for the jack. The truck sank. Lee pulled out the jack and moved down the truck.

'You couldn't pay me to stand up in that hat,' said Bruce.

Gary lit another joint. He looked over at Bruce who was staring through the last of the amber liquid at the sun. 'Spent the winter in a boarding house down the road from the shop,' Bruce said, rolling to expose his broad white side and the symmetrical welt there. 'I had my bed too close to the radiator.' He drained the bottle and stood using Gary's shoulder as a prop. 'People underestimate the cold in Canterbury.'

Gary thought about Adelaide again, then the pressure in his bladder and then Tania. Sometimes, when he got home from his shift she'd bring him a beer she'd chilled in the freezer. The can would be ice cold to hold and the beer itself would be on the brink of freezing. 'A beer blizzard,' he said, unsure what he meant by it.

But Bruce hadn't heard. He was watching Lee who'd come around the truck and was holding his hands out in a question.

'A record,' said Gary exultantly.

Lee raised his fists and made a circle so that he was facing the truck.

Bruce hurled the bottle. It missed Lee, hitting the front tyre with a dead thud. Bruce sat and then lay down quickly so that his feet went up with the momentum. Lee hadn't noticed. He was leaning on the truck looking at the pig.

'He didn't see,' said Gary, taking a deep hit. He started to say something about fresh starts, or at least started to think about saying something about fresh starts.

Bruce held up his hand and made his all-knowing face. He pointed through the grass at Lee who was still staring at the pig. 'Picks me up every Sunday – takes me to the supermarket so I can do my shopping. He's done it ever since I started.'

Gary exhaled and then straight away took another hit. He noticed that his hand was on the bulge his wallet made in his trousers. He thought hard about what it all meant. 'Today's a Sunday,' he said, after a while.